**ROSES. LIMOS. TUXES. DRAMA.
WELCOME TO THE MOST IMPORTANT
NIGHT OF THE YEAR.**

Tara knew what would happen if she showed up to the prom solo. Nisha and Jordan would make the extra effort to include her, but as the night progressed, the slow tunes would certainly outweigh the fast ones. Eventually Jordan and Nate would casually disappear for some alone time while Nisha and Brian remained glued to the dance floor, losing themselves in each other's eyes. And what would Tara be doing? She'd be feeling pretty awkward as she watched over her friends' sparkly evenings bags—back at the table, alone. No, going to the prom stag was definitely out of the question.

"Maybe I should forget about the dress now," Tara said. "What I really need to do is focus on finding the right guy."

Read all the **Prom** books!

ONCE UPON A PROM #1

ONCE UPON A PROM #2

ONCE UPON A PROM #3
date

Also by Jeanine Le Ny

I ♥ BIKINIS: ISLAND SUMMER

ONCE UPON A PROM

dream

JEANINE LE NY

Point

ISBN 13: 978-0-545-02815-8
ISBN 10: 0-545-02815-9

Copyright © 2008 by Jeanine Le Ny
All rights reserved. Published by Scholastic Inc.

SCHOLASTIC, POINT, and associated logos are trademarks and/or registered trademarks of Scholastic Inc.

Text design by Steve Scott.

12 11 10 9 8 7 6 5 4 3 2 1   8 9 10 11 12 13/0

Printed in the U.S.A.
First printing, February 2008

For my parents, especially Mom, who had the good sense not *to let me buy that poufy red prom dress no matter how awesome my "friend" said I looked in it.*
—JLN

Acknowledgments

An enormous thanks goes to Abby McAden who encouraged my grand foray into author-hood; my wonderful editor, Aimee Friedman, for her superb guidance, grace, and humor; Segal Manoj for her invaluable insight on growing up Indian in America; and of course, my husband, Gencer, for his limitless supply of support, understanding, and *borek*.

ONCE UPON A PROM

dream

CHAPTER *One*

"Now, *this* is the mother of all prom dresses," seventeen-year-old Jordan Taylor declared in the Nordstrom dressing salon at the mall. She swept aside the pink velvet curtain of her changing stall and emerged wearing a hideously *Carmen*esque red satin cocktail number complete with flouncing purple petticoat and matching fake flower for the hair. Swinging her skirts, she sashayed across the carpet, giving her best friend, Nisha Khubani, the full effect of the outfit.

Nisha laughed at Jordan's getup from atop a square pedestal in the main area of the dressing room. "If we were having an

1

ugliest dress contest, you'd *so* be the winner right now," she said.

"I know!" Jordan giggled, catching her gaudy image in the wall of mirrors. "It's so awful, I couldn't resist trying it on." She wasn't sure if it was the excitement over prom season or because she'd just led the Emerson High cheerleading squad to victory at Nationals, but Jordan was feeling giddy. She piled her shoulder-length blond hair on top of her head and stuck her tongue out at herself.

Nisha flipped her long dark tresses to one side and examined the sweet pale-yellow empire gown with satin spaghetti straps that she was wearing. Jordan thought the dress looked striking against Nisha's latte-colored skin. "It's gorgeous," she commented.

"Thanks. I must have tried it on a million times but, I don't know . . ." Nisha squinted at her reflection. "I guess it's still a definite maybe," she replied, stepping down from the pedestal. "What about the white gown you picked out, Jordan? I'm dying to see it on you."

"I was saving that one for last," Jordan admitted and headed back to the heap of rejects flung over the chair in her changing room: a swingy mauve-and-black knee-length dress that was too cutesy; a fitted coral micro-mini that looked hot on the hanger but, once on, had "wardrobe malfunction" written all over it; and a low-cut sparkly blue gown that kind of made her feel pageant-like — and not in a good way.

Peeling off the silly cha-cha dress, Jordan added it to the top of the pile. Then she carefully removed the one-shouldered white silk gown from its hanger and slipped it on over her head. As soon as she felt the cool fabric slide luxuriously down her skin, she knew it was going to be good. Nisha's reaction when Jordan came out of the changing stall confirmed it.

"Whoa," Nisha breathed, now in a lacy black halter dress that didn't quite suit her.

"It's, like, you're glowing or something, Jordan."

"Really?" Jordan quickly stepped onto the pedestal to catch herself in the three-way mirror. Simple and elegant, the silky white material skimmed lightly over her curves, ending just above her pedicured toes, and it really *did* seem to brighten her alabaster skin tone. "Ooh, I love it," she said with a flutter of excitement. "It reminds me of something an old-time starlet might have worn to the Academy Awards!"

"You have to get it," Nisha said as Jordan pointed her right foot to the side, exposing a long, lean leg through the high slit in the skirt.

Jordan smiled. She felt exactly the same way. "Hey Tara, hurry up and get out here. I think I just found my prom dress!" she called to her other best friend — who seemed to have gotten stuck in her changing stall — as Nisha nudged Jordan aside to get a view in the mirror.

Tara Macmillan peeked out from behind her own velvet curtain, displaying only a delicate pale face framed by her chocolate-brown waves. She spied Jordan's dress and sighed dramatically. "You look *amazing*," she said with a hint of irritation in her voice.

"Gee, thanks, Tara," Jordan replied, planting her hands on her hips. "I'm really feeling the love right now."

"No, the dress is super-beautiful," Tara said. "It's just . . . I can't believe you found the perfect thing on your first day of shopping, when Nisha and I have been searching for *weeks*. It's not fair!"

What could Jordan say? Between practicing for Nationals and seeing her boyfriend, she'd been too busy to prom shop until today — and finding the ideal gown *had* been freakishly easy. And, as Tara liked to say, that was the story of Jordan's life. Jordan didn't need to study too much to score excellent grades, and her successful cheerleading career began at age eleven when a coach saw her perform a backflip as a lark in gym. Then there was Jordan's long-time and totally hot in that buff-captain-of-every-team-sort-of-way boyfriend, Nate Lombardo, who was smitten after only a casual glance from Jordan while she was traveling between French and AP American History.

But the luckiest moment of Jordan's life had been meeting Nisha and Tara. The three of them had become instant BFFs the moment they'd sat next to one another in Mrs. Berry's second-grade classroom. Now they were so inseparable that it was difficult for Jordan to imagine life without them — even though she knew she'd be living it in just a few months when they all headed off to different colleges.

"Okay, you guys, tell me what you think of this." Tara came out of her changing room, revealing a short, taupe-colored, taffeta bubble dress. "Is it me, or what?" She did a quick twirl, puffing out the skirt, subsequently making the dress resemble a large upside-down mushroom.

Nisha turned from the mirror. "Oh, that's classic!" she said with a snort.

"It may not be *your* style, Nisha, but I like it," Tara said in that defiant tone she got whenever frustrated. "It's cute — in a 1980s retro sort of way — and funky." She turned to Jordan. "Am I right?"

How could Jordan put it tactfully? "Um, remember those silly pictures my mom showed us of *her* prom? It was when? In, like, 1985 or something? The gigantic hair . . . those puffy pastel dresses?"

"So you're saying I look stupid?" Tara asked, raising one hand to flatten her curls as the other crinkled the fabric of her skirt.

"No, no," Jordan replied quickly, not exactly understanding why Tara was being so sensitive all of a sudden. But then again, Tara sometimes took herself a bit too seriously when she was stressed. And Tara *did* have a lot on her plate. Being the head of the prom committee, she was responsible for pulling together the most awesome party Emerson High had ever seen.

Nisha hopped off the pedestal to join the girls. "Listen, Tara, eighties retro is cool in theory, but I'm telling you, ten years from now we're all going to regret being so fashion-conscious. Case in point — I was totally traumatized when I found out what my butt *really* looks like in my skinny jeans," she said, gently guiding Tara toward the three-way mirror.

"What are you talking about?" Jordan asked, following them. "You look fine to me in those jeans, Nisha."

Nisha rolled her eyes. "You're sweet, Jordan, but there's a difference between being *passable* in skinny jeans and looking *unbelievably hot* like you do in yours."

"Tell me about it," Tara agreed. "She eats like a guy, and she's still a rail."

Jordan felt a slight blush creep onto her cheeks. "I can't help it if I have an abnormally fast metabolism," she said in her own defense. Besides, it wasn't as if her two friends weren't rock stars in their own right. Nisha was so pretty and petite, and her thick luxurious hair and mysterious almond-shaped eyes were definitely to be envied. And Tara possessed that strong, regal kind of beauty that totally freaked out cute boys, transforming them into aloof mutes too scared to speak to her. (Miraculously, and unfortunately for Tara, the not-so-cute boys often had no fear.) Sure, Jordan knew she was a bit more popular with guys than her friends were but that was only because she was an everyday-type of hottie. Beautiful yet approachable. The kind of girl that heads cheerleading squads and stars in toothpaste commercials and is not the least bit exotic. Jordan shook off the thought.

"Anyway," Nisha went on, positioning Tara so that her back was toward the mirror. "I'm assuming that you guys haven't been to Cynthia Camdin's MySpace page lately. The pictures from her party are up, and there's an extreme close-up of a certain girl's butt in a certain pair of skinny jeans.

Let's just say I recognized the jeans — and it wasn't pretty. At all."

"So, the moral of the story?" Tara asked.

"Always go shopping with a pocket mirror," Jordan cracked.

"Gold star for the future prom queen," Nisha said, grinning at Jordan. "No really. I'm not kidding." She handed Tara her compact and pointed to the full-length mirror. "Now look," she ordered her.

Tara opened Nisha's compact and gazed into the tiny mirror, which reflected a bulbous image behind her. It didn't take long for her big brown eyes to register the horror. "Oh. My. *God*. My butt. It looks gigantic!" She turned this way and that to glimpse the different angles then gaped back at Jordan and Nisha. "You guys are such good friends," she said solemnly. "I mean it. Really, *really* good friends."

Jordan slung an arm around Tara's shoulders. "That's what we're here for. If you can't trust your best friends to help pick out your prom dress, who *can* you trust?"

*　*　*

Exactly twenty-three minutes later, Jordan had bought the white gown, Nisha had put the yellow one on hold, and Tara had decided to drown her sorrows in a plate of delicious cheese-smothered fries in the food court.

"I don't know, I guess I'm just not convinced that Brian will love me in yellow," Nisha said, sipping her mango-raspberry smoothie. "It's such a special night. I really want to look great for him, you know?"

"That's so cute," Jordan said, sipping on her Coke. So was Brian Schroder, Nisha's boyfriend of nearly six months. The two of them were, by far, one of the most adorable couples at school and probably would have been voted "Most Likely to Live Happily Ever After" in the yearbook had Jordan and *her* BF, Nate, not been bestowed the honor.

As if on cue, Jordan noticed some baseball players in their Emerson Cougars T-shirts entering the food court like a tidal wave of purple and white. Leading them was a tall, lean, sandy-haired boy with an irresistible smile.

Nate. He waved to her.

Jordan waved back, noticing that he was looking particularly delicious today in his varsity jacket. "Nate's here," she said to her friends, motioning across the court. "Do you guys mind? I've got to talk to him about Friday night. We're going to a movie at the indie theater downtown. I found a French one that seems cool."

"French?" Tara asked, waving a cheese fry. "Since when are you guys into foreign flicks?"

"Since now," Jordan said with a shrug. "Actually, I just wanted to try something new. I'm sick of the whole same-party-different-house thing, and Nate said we could do whatever I wanted this weekend."

"Aw, Nate's such a good boyfriend," Nisha said.

"He *is*," Jordan agreed, knowing that her movie choice probably wasn't Nate's idea of a good time since (a) it was shot in black and white, (b) it was subtitled, (c) he'd have to wear his glasses to *read* the subtitles, and (d) the movie would not include one solitary explosion. She grabbed a couple of fries and slid back her chair. "Later, ladies." She blew her friends a kiss, gathered the garment bag with her gown in it, and crossed the food court to where Nate was sitting with his buddies.

"Hey," Nate said, pulling her onto his lap and kissing her as a soundtrack of "awwwww"s played from the other guys on the team.

Jordan smiled and slipped her arms around her boyfriend's waist, nestling her head onto his broad shoulder and breathing in the faint yet familiar fragrance of his Irish Spring soap. Just being around Nate seemed to relax Jordan. He had a way of making her feel as if everything was going to be okay — even when nothing was wrong.

"What's up?" she asked the group, not caring that she'd just morphed into a mushy, cuddly blob in front of them.

"You guys are, like, so sweet!" a sophomore girl with a jet-black ponytail exclaimed. She playfully swatted the arm of the beefy Emerson catcher who was in the chair beside her. "Moose, how come you're not this cute with me?" she demanded. Apparently Moose had finally found himself a girlfriend.

Moose leaned toward her. "C'mere, babe!" he said, with his arms — and lips — outstretched.

The girl giggled and squirmed as Moose gave her a big, fat, juicy kiss on the cheek. "You are so gross!" she said, wiping her face and laughing along with everyone.

"So you guys are going to Sam's party tomorrow night, right?" Billy MacIntyre, the first baseman, asked as he raked back his thick blond hair with a hand.

"Can't make it," Jordan replied.

At the same time, Nate said, "We're there, bro."

"But we're going to the movies," Jordan reminded Nate. "I picked a French one called *Vert et Vrai*. You promised you'd take me, remember?"

"That's tomorrow? Oh, *man*! I thought that was *next* week." Nate slapped his forehead with his hand, which seemed staged to Jordan. "Man!"

She squinted at Nate. "Oh, my God. You are *so* trying to get out of seeing the movie," she realized aloud.

"What? No! No way. I totally want to go," Nate said as he was clearly going down in flames. He looked from Jordan to Billy to Moose, and then back at Jordan.

"Dude, you can't miss the celebration," Billy broke in. "Sam's parents are out of town this week, and Sam and his sister are getting a band. It'll be the party of the century, for sure."

Just like last week's was and the week before that, too? Jordan wondered. Besides, as far as she was concerned, their senior prom would hold that title.

15

"I know we've gone to a lot of jock parties," Nate said as if reading her mind, "but high school is ending soon, and who knows when we'll get to see these guys after we start college." He regarded Jordan with his soft, chestnut-colored eyes. "Maybe we can go see *Vertebrae,* or whatever it's called, on Saturday?"

"It's *Vert et Vrai,*" Jordan said, holding back a smile. And there *was* one more showing on Saturday afternoon she knew, but what about the principle of the situation?

"Think about it, Jordan . . . *a band,*" Moose put in, trying to win her over, but Jordan rolled her eyes.

"Wait. A band?" Nate said as if he was hearing it for the first time. "Jordan, did you hear that? Now we have to go." Jordan shrieked as Nate surprised her by standing up, then swooping her off her feet. "A band, Jord. Come on, you have to say yes to a band."

He looked so cute and wide-eyed as he smiled up at her. And his teammates were all staring, waiting for an answer.

"You're such a goofball," Jordan told Nate, shaking her head. "Okay, let's go to the party." She turned to Moose. "And that band had better be *good*."

"Yeah!" Moose howled as the others laughed.

Nate lowered Jordan, then barraged her with ticklish pecks on the neck and cheeks. When he came to Jordan's lips he paused. "You're the best, Jord," he whispered, his face inches from hers. "We'll go see your movie on Saturday, I promise, okay?"

"Mmm-hmm," Jordan whispered back, knowing that Nate was sincere. She tilted her head slightly before their lips joined in a soft kiss, and Jordan savored the moment.

So what if her boyfriend wasn't into experimental films or art exhibits or anything that strayed too far from sports?

Jordan decided she wasn't going to ruin the end of senior year — or the upcoming, magical thrill of prom — by focusing on Nate's flaws. And the boy was still willing to see a movie, which he would undoubtedly dislike, because he loved her. If Nate was able to compromise, so was she.

CHAPTER *Two*

Prom Date Candidates (B-List)

1) **JOE:**   *Nice bod. Luvs Grey Poupon . . .
a LOT. Serious halitosis.
Suggest curiously strong breath
mints?*

2) **ROBERT:**   *OMG beautiful. Asked Jordan to
Prom twice before me. Not that
desperate . . . yet.*

3) **DARREN:**   *Very cute and sweet. Constantly
chewing the same toothpick. Weird
dental obsession? Possible therapy
before Prom?*

Put down *the cheese fry,* Tara told herself as she stared at the luscious potato dripping with gooey melted cheddar. But she popped it into her mouth anyway. It was totally unrealistic to expect herself to resist a perfectly good plate of fries, especially when Nisha was there to save her from wolfing down the whole thing.

Besides, Tara needed to keep up her energy. How else was she going to find the ideal prom dress — let alone a hot, smart, funny, athletic, and modest boy to beg her to attend the prom with him? As it was, the contenders were looking pretty slim: zero hotties on her A-list, three B-listers, and half the school's male upperclass population on the No-Way-in-Heck list. And, although Tara would never admit it to anyone, she was beginning to worry that she'd *never* find the right date for the prom.

"What's up?" Nisha asked, shaking Tara out of her thoughts. "You're so quiet."

"Oh, just thinking about the prom," Tara replied. "What else?" She was just about to go for another fry when her combination phone and handheld computer chirped out the tune of Beethoven's Ninth Symphony. Tara groaned, knowing it could be only one person on the other end of that ringtone. She picked up her handheld from its spot on the table and pressed MUTE, letting the call go to voice mail.

"I swear, Jenny Brigger joined the prom committee for the sole purpose of torturing me," Tara declared. "Now she's insisting we 'rethink' the theme. She's probably calling to bug me about it before our meeting on Monday."

"I thought that was settled." Nisha sipped her smoothie. "Didn't you say we were doing *Starry Night*?"

"That's what I *thought* when I made the executive decision," Tara said, nodding. She'd pictured the ballroom at the Fairmont Hotel draped in the blues and greens and golds from the famous Van Gogh painting, with tons of colorful round Chinese lanterns hanging over the dance floor. "Then Jenny went to the principal to complain because I nixed all of her lame ideas, and he's got this thing about working as a team, blah, blah, blah. . . . Anyway, I can't believe she's pulling this when she *knows* that I've got more pressing matters."

"Like what?" Nisha asked. "What's more pressing than planning the prom?"

Tara gave her friend a serious look. "Hello? Were you not there shopping right next to me today? You know I'm a week behind schedule in the dress department and now I'm . . ." She paused to check her handheld. ". . . three weeks late finding a cute guy to form a meaningful relationship with before P-day."

"You've got to be kidding, Tara. You don't *really* have that on your checklist, do you?" Nisha asked. "I mean, we'll all have a great time no matter who we go with . . . or don't go with."

"It's the prom, Nisha," Tara said, nibbling on another fry. "I wouldn't kid." Especially since she knew what would happen if she showed up solo. Of course Nisha and Jordan would make the extra effort to include her, but as the night progressed the slow tunes would certainly outweigh the fast ones. Eventually Jordan and Nate would casually disappear for some alone time while Nisha and Brian remained glued to the dance floor, swaying and losing themselves in each other's eyes until the DJ spun out the last dreamy song of the night. And what would Tara be doing? She'd be feeling pretty awkward as she watched over her friends' sparkly evening bags — back at the table, alone. No, going to the prom stag was definitely out of the question.

"Maybe I should forget about the dress for now," Tara said. "What I really need to do is focus on finding the right guy. I'll give myself another week. That should be enough time, no?"

Nisha laughed. "Girl, if anybody can do it, you can." She checked her cell phone, then slid back her chair and stood. "Gotta bolt. I have just enough time to meet Brian at American Eagle, then head home."

"So you're leaving me here alone with the fries?" Tara asked, incredulous. "I'll eat them all and get a ton of zits. Who's going to want to go to the prom with me then? My lists will be totally irrelevant."

"Um, stressed much?" Nisha asked as she snatched her pink backpack off a chair and hitched it onto a shoulder. "Sorry, sweetie. You know how my parents get when I'm late." Natives of India, Mr. and Mrs. Khubani were notoriously conservative, turning the words "overprotective parents" into a major understatement.

Okay, so maybe I am *a little tense about the prom*, Tara thought, watching Nisha weave through the maze of tables, then disappear. But the thought of being the fifth wheel at what was supposed to be the most romantic night of a teen girl's life made her stomach churn. She pushed away the plate of fries and rested her chin in her hands. *And maybe I'm being too picky, like my friends are always telling me. I guess I could just settle for whatever.*

Trying her best not to feel like a total diva, Tara scanned the possibilities on her B-list yet again, but a familiar shriek of laughter broke through the din of the food court and rudely interrupted her thought process. She glanced up to see Jordan and the baseball crew horsing around. Nate had just grabbed a squirming Jordan and lifted her up in his muscular arms. Then they proceeded to laugh and play-wrestle as if they were starring in their very own Abercrombie & Fitch ad.

How come Jordan *never has to settle for anything?* Tara thought, feeling a surge of unwanted envy as she glanced away from the scene. It was true that Jordan was Tara's best friend but sometimes, especially on days like today, Tara couldn't help hating the girl.

No. Hate is a strong word. You. Do. Not. *Hate. Jordan. Taylor.* Tara reminded herself. Lately it had become a daily affirmation. No, no. She couldn't hate Jordan. How could she? Jordan, along with Nisha, was a real friend who'd always had Tara's back — from the time she helped Tara stand up to Tabitha Spraig in the second grade to, well, not letting Tara buy an unflattering dress for the prom. Tara and Jordan had been tight since forever — at least until Nate came along.

Tara forced another peek at Jordan and her boyfriend's blissful display of perfection. Eyes closed, arms entwined, Jordan and Nate were now kissing in front of the entire mall. And, of course, the sunlight streaming in from the skylight above the food court was catching Jordan's sleek hair just so, making it appear even blonder and shinier than usual. *Why does Jordan feel the need to rub her happiness in everybody's face?* Tara wondered bitterly. *And how in God's name could someone look so glamorous in a pair of jeans and couple of layered tees?*

Actually, Jordan was so tall and gorgeous that Tara wouldn't be surprised if next week some model scout (a real one, not the creepy guy who walked around the Galleria with a camera and a few business cards) "discovered" Jordan and whisked her away to Milan or Paris or some other exciting place that regular people only dream about. Tara closed her eyes, trying to picture Selina, Illinois — their sleepy little suburb about an hour outside of Chicago — sans Jordan Taylor and couldn't decide if it would be cool or completely devastating. Like most things in Tara's life, her feelings about Jordan were complicated.

Tara didn't *want* to be jealous of her best friend. Really. Who did? But still, how could it possibly be fair for one girl, namely Jordan, to have absolutely *everything* going for her? Jordan was not only beautiful and smart, she was *nice*, too, and admired by guys and girls alike. Her friend was so popular that Tara saw no point in running for prom queen herself — even though she'd been putting her heart and soul into planning the event — since Jordan was certain to win the title.

If that weren't enough, Jordan's gorgeous boyfriend, Nate, was the Cougars' first-string quarterback in the fall and played right field for the baseball team in the spring, which kind of made him a shoo-in for prom king.

Let's contrast that with me and my nonexistent love life, Tara thought wryly. Sure, she'd gone on a couple of dates. Tara knew she was smart and not in the least bit shy — especially when it came to the opposite sex. So why was it that Tara hadn't had a steady since the two-month Charlie Bosworth debacle back in sophomore year? Which, now that she contemplated it, probably didn't even count since she and Charlie had never officially kissed.

Tara sighed and observed as Nate whispered something to Jordan that made her smile. *God, he must be so romantic,* Tara thought. *I'd kill to have a dreamy guy like Nate. Or even a* date *with a guy like Nate. . . .* She sighed, deciding that she'd spent enough time feeling sorry for herself. Tired of the dark place she was in and thankful to have the sense to keep the sporadic pity parties to herself, Tara turned away from the couple for the last time. Maybe she should go home — do some schoolwork, have the obligatory dinner with the parents, surf the Web looking for prom dresses, then soak in a luxurious bubble bath before bed for a little mind-clearing "me time."

Tara was about to head out when her cell phone chirped to let her know someone had sent her a text message. She scrolled her handheld to view the message, hoping that it wasn't that Jenny from the prom committee again. Tara was in no mood. She clicked open the text with her stylus:

Hi! Those fries look good. Can I have 1?
   — K
PS: U R the prettiest gurl here

Tara tried to play it cool, but felt her heart skip a beat as she read the text again, then glanced at her plate of fries. *Someone thinks I'm hot!*

But who was *K*? Tara wondered, quickly flipping through the files in her brain for a familiar name starting with the initial, hoping to think of a cute boy that she'd totally forgotten about. She felt like an excited schoolgirl, which she had every right to do since technically she still was . . . for about another month or so.

Wait a sec, she thought as something horrible occurred to her. *Could this be . . . a joke?* Possibly. Pranks like this were known to happen. Usually to *other* people, but Tara wasn't willing to chance humiliation. She casually inspected the kids in the food court to see if anyone was laughing or slightly smirking in her direction.

Nope. No one was paying her the slightest bit of attention. This was good. Very good. No, wait. Not good. How was she supposed to figure out who K was if he wasn't even looking at her?

She had to go logical for a minute.

Step 1: Check where the text came from. Tara clicked open the text's information box with her stylus. But instead of a cell phone number popping up, the word RESTRICTED was there. Which sucked.

Step 2: Try texting back. She typed the reply, *WHO R U?* and tried to send it, but the text wouldn't go through because the number was restricted. *Duh*, she thought. *So much for logical. Now what?*

She scanned the food court again, this time hoping that some unbelievable hottie — preferably a college guy — was giving her the eye. Otherwise there was no way for her to find out his identity. Unless —

Beeeeeeeeep!

He'd texted her again!

Tara could hardly contain her glee as she clicked open the message, which said:

C u in skool 2morrow!

    — K (ur c-kret admirer)

Oh, well. Not a college guy, Tara realized. *But somebody at school actually has a crush on me?* She smiled to herself, letting the thought sink in. It didn't take long before a few other ideas popped into her head.

Maybe he's cute. Maybe he's sweet. Maybe I'll snag a hot date to the prom after all!

CHAPTER *Three*

Nisha closed her eyes and wrapped her arms around her boyfriend, Brian, as she pressed her lips to his. She didn't want to let go but knew she'd have to. Eventually.

Nisha and Brian hadn't planned on kissing in his car before he dropped her off, but somehow, lately, it had been getting more and more difficult to say good-bye. It was only last November when they'd started dating, but Nisha could hardly remember what life was like before Brian. Now they were coming up on their six-month anniversary!

Finally, the two parted and Nisha wondered what her Indian-born parents would think if they knew that she had kissed her American boyfriend with abandon in front of Wegmans. *They'd freak,* she thought. *On several levels.* She pushed the thought to the back of her mind, though, when Brian took her hand in his.

"So I was thinking . . . instead of taking old Diablo here to the prom, maybe we should go in style. Like, in a limo. Just the two of us." He tapped the dashboard of his red Honda Civic. "No offense, Diablo."

"Are you serious?" Nisha asked, doing a little clap and bouncing in her seat. She'd ridden in a limousine with her parents for her older sister Kali's wedding last year, but the thought of her and Brian traveling to the prom in one seemed so absolutely, positively, undeniably *romantic.* "It's perfect!" she cried.

"Anything for my girl," Brian said, acting all nonchalant. "Plus my parents offered to help out with it. How could I say no?" he added, his blue eyes twinkling. Nisha couldn't resist kissing him again.

"So, did you have fun with Jordan and Tara at the mall?" he asked. "Get anything good?"

"Well, actually, there *is* this one dress that I put on hold at Nordstrom." Nisha then proceeded to describe the yellow empire in precise detail from the satin spaghetti straps with the teeny bows on them to the shimmery chiffon skirt to the reservations she had about the color. "I don't know. Do you like yellow? It's not mustard yellow or a goldish yellow or anything like that. It's softer. Kind of like, um, *this*." She rifled in her backpack, pulled out the special prom edition of *Seventeen*, and pointed to the cover girl's pale dress. When she was finished, she noticed that Brian was staring at her with that charming grin of his. "What?" she asked.

"Nothing," he said, but by now his smile was taking up the entire lower region of his face. "It's just cute how you're getting so excited about the prom."

"Aren't *you* excited?" Nisha asked.

Brian nodded and reached out to sweep away a few stray hairs from Nisha's eyes. "Just don't make me wear a tie and cummerbund to match your dress. Got it?" he teased.

"Got it," Nisha said with a giggle. Then she glimpsed the time on the dashboard clock and gasped. She had exactly four minutes to get home, and she was still three blocks away from her house. "Uh-oh. I've got to run, Brian," she said, giving him a quick peck on the lips and opening the car door. "My mom's expecting me."

"Are you sure you want me to leave you here?" Brian asked, concerned. "Why don't I just take you to your house?"

Nisha glanced at the supermarket they were parked in front of. "Um, that's okay. I've got to buy something here," she told him, which was a total lie, but what was she supposed to say? Nisha didn't have the heart to tell Brian that her parents would flip if they knew she was dating — let alone dating a boy who wasn't Indian. In fact, going to the prom with Brian was going to be a *major* undertaking, but Nisha couldn't think about that just yet.

"I can wait for you if you want," Brian said as Nisha climbed out of the car.

"Oh, that's all right," Nisha told him. "It's only a block or two. I'll IM you later, all right?"

"Um, okay," Brian said with a shrug.

Nisha closed the car door and pretended to enter the supermarket as Brian drove away. When the coast was clear, she turned and hurried down the street to her house. *This is getting harder,* Nisha thought, making a quick left off the main road. *Brian knows I'm being weird, but he doesn't know why.*

When she'd first started seeing Brian it had been easy not to invite him to her home because, let's face it, no boy wanted to meet his girlfriend's parents — especially in the beginning of a relationship. But lately, as odd as it was for the male species, Brian had begun hinting that he wanted to come over by shooting her casual lines such as, "I'll pick you up — at your house" or "So what's for dinner tonight?"

Nisha totally wanted to introduce her boyfriend to her parents. Really. She'd even practiced the whole Brian-these-are-the-parents/parents-this-is-Brian scene in front of the full-length mirror in her bedroom, but she knew it wouldn't work. Stuff just didn't go down like that back in India.

In India, Nisha knew, girls and guys didn't usually date; they got engaged. Americans didn't get engaged until *after* dating . . . well, except maybe for the couples who got married by Elvis impersonators in Vegas, but that was beside the point. And although Nisha had been living in America since she was six and *felt* one hundred percent American, her parents (mostly her mom) were constantly reminding her that she wasn't. "Just because we are Americans does not mean that we can turn our backs on where we came from, Nisha," her mother was always telling her. "We can never forget India."

Nisha didn't want to turn her back on India. She just wanted to tweak the rules a little to fit in with her American lifestyle, that was all. *Yeah, right. Like that would ever happen*, she thought.

Nisha's family was so traditional that last year, after her sister Kali graduated from medical school, their mom and dad arranged for Kali to marry an Indian boy — Dutta Wadhwa — who was a software engineer based in London, which was where Kali was living now. Dutta seemed like a nice guy to Nisha, and her mother was always talking about how he came from an excellent family. The wedding ceremony was a grand event, with both families and their friends celebrating at an estate just outside of Mumbai. Nisha had marveled at the thousands of yellow lilies brought in solely for the occasion, and she'd never seen her sister look more stunning than she had on that day. Kali had been adorned head-to-toe in flowing red silk, with a beautiful bejeweled headpiece trickling gracefully down her forehead. Golden bangles stacked her wrists, and an intricate henna design swirled across her hands and feet. And Kali had been happy. Really happy. Everyone was — including Nisha, who'd danced like a Bollywood star for almost three days straight.

Tradition seemed to have worked out for Kali, and Nisha certainly wouldn't mind visiting her sister in London over the summer. So maybe her parents were right about not letting Nisha date. Finding a partner should be left to elders who knew better, right?

There was one not-so-tiny problem that kept niggling around in Nisha's head. Unlike her sister, Nisha could never wrap her mind around the concept of "learning to love your husband." *How is that possible?* she wondered. *What if one day you wake up and realize that you don't love him — and that you never will?*

No, someday Nisha wanted to marry a man that she was madly, deeply, and passionately *in love* with — not just some nice guy from a good family.

As she approached her home, Nisha wrapped her locks into a neat ponytail to avoid the *why-is-your-hair-always-in-your-face* argument and opened the front door. She was instantly greeted by the delicious aroma of the *garam masala* spices her mother often cooked with. Nisha had to admit that although not being one hundred percent American had its complications, home-cooked Indian food was definitely not one of them. She placed her backpack on the floor by the door and slipped out of her Skechers. Then she crossed the hall into the kitchen to find her mother standing by the stove, apron tied around her dark blue sari, stirring up her famous *gobi aloo*, a delectable potato-and-cauliflower curry.

"Hi, Mommy." Nisha kissed her mother's cheek, breathing in the garlic-ginger scent emanating from the pot. "Mmmm. Dinner smells delish. Dad's going to be one happy man tonight," she remarked. *Gobi aloo* was his favorite vegetable dish. Nisha's, too. She swiped a piece of spicy cauliflower with her fingers and popped it into her mouth.

"Nisha! What is this? Who taught you your manners?" Her mother glared at her for a second, then softened. "How is it? Enough turmeric?"

Nisha laughed. "It's awesome, Mom," she said.

"I'm making lamb *biriyani*, too." Mrs. Khubani gestured toward the oven. "You and your father are *very* lucky," she said with an infectious smile. She opened the oven to check the lamb. "Tell me, how was your day at school, *Beta*?" she asked, using her pet name for Nisha. Roughly translated, it meant "sweetheart" in Hindi.

"Oh, you know. The same." Nisha hitched up onto the countertop and watched her mother add onions and a few red chilies to the *gobi aloo*, which got Nisha thinking. Her father was sure to be in a good mood after eating his favorite meal. Maybe tonight was the right time to broach the subject of the prom . . . cautiously, of course.

It'd been a long time since Nisha had brought up the topic of boys in the Khubani household. It wasn't worth the argument anymore. Her parents had a hard enough time understanding why it was so important for Nisha to wear the right clothes, sleep over at her friends' houses, and spend countless hours on the Internet — just like every other girl her age did. They'd never get the whole bringing-a-date-to-the-prom thing. Even if they did, their old-fashioned customs would never allow it.

So what was an American girl, who happened to have been born in India, to do?

Nisha had it down to a science. Getting permission to attend an event of this magnitude was a process and needed to be done in stages.

First, she'd mention the dance to her mother. Then Mom would tell her father about it. Approximately one week later, Nisha would casually say that the event was formal and that she might need something fancy to wear. Under no circumstances would Nisha reference boys, slow dancing, flowers, limos, or dates. If either one asked, she'd say that she was going with friends, which wasn't technically a lie. Brian was a friend — a very *close* friend — and Nisha and Brian would be sitting at a table with Jordan and Nate and Tara and her date. *Friends.*

"*Beta*, it's time to set the table," Mrs. Khubani said. "Your father should be home soon. At least I hope so. The *gobi aloo* will be ready in fifteen minutes."

Nisha slid off the countertop and removed the plates from a cabinet, carefully phrasing her next sentence. "Actually, something interesting *did* happen at school today," she said, trying to sound casual as she placed the dishes around the kitchen table. "There was an announcement about this event . . . it's called the prom."

"Prom?" Her mother turned. "What is this 'prom'?" They didn't have proms in

India, Nisha knew, which was to her advantage.

She opened a drawer and picked out some utensils. "It's just this party that the school is having for the graduating class," she replied with a shrug.

"Oh. That sounds nice." Mrs. Khubani turned back to the stove to give the *gobi aloo* another stir.

Nisha understood the importance of her next sentence. It had to be uttered just so. No inflection, no inference of hope equals no suspicions.

The prom should in no way appear as if it was a big deal.

"So . . ." she asked, almost sounding bored, "do you think Dad will let me go?"

The process was set in motion.

CHAPTER *Four*

Famous Guys With "K" Names

1) Kevin Federline (loser)
2) Keith Urban (taken and, anyway, sings country music)
3) Kanye West (cute, but has thing for gold diggers)
4) Kid Rock (ew)
5) Karl Marx (creepy . . . and dead)
6) Kiefer Sutherland (old, yet somewhat talented)
7) Keanu Reeves (just plain old)
8) Kap'n Krunch? (delish, but check spelling)
9) Krad Pitt? Kustin Timberlake? Korlando Bloom?

46

"Why is it that all the celebrity guys that have a name starting with 'K' are either gross or totally old or something?" Tara pondered aloud during lunch the next afternoon.

"Huh?" Nisha stared at Tara from across the table, a perplexed expression on her face and a spoonful of strawberry yogurt halfway to her mouth.

"What does that have to do with anything?" Jordan asked from beside Nisha, flipping through one of Nisha's prom magazines and looking adorable in her white-and-purple cheerleading uniform.

Tara could see how her question might seem random, considering that Nisha had just finished explaining to Tara and Jordan the expertly orchestrated start of her prom plan — which was great but did absolutely nothing to solve Tara's dilemma. Maybe it was time to share.

"I have some news of my own," Tara explained. "Yesterday, after you guys left your best friend all alone to hang with your *boy*friends, someone sent me a few texts." She opened her black leather satchel, pulled out her handheld, and showed her friends said messages.

Nisha snatched the phone out of Tara's hand. "Oh, my God. You have a secret admirer. This is so exciting!" she cried. "I'll bet he's going to ask you to the prom!"

"Hold on a sec," Tara said, swiping back her precious phone — she really didn't like other people touching it if she could help it — and scanned the message for the zillionth time. "I'd like to know who 'K' *is* first, before we go to the prom together."

"That's probably a good idea," Jordan said. "Let's start with your list, Tara. I'm assuming you have one, right?" She grinned at her friend.

"Sort of." Tara slid over her AP English notebook, where she'd compiled her celebrity K-list last period. "I couldn't think of anybody at school, so I made this. I'm really hoping Korlando Bloom has the crush on me, but somehow I don't think it's going to turn out that way," she said, and then bit into her chicken salad sandwich.

"*I* know who it could be," Nisha piped in. "What about that guy on Yearbook, Kobe Finnegan?"

Tara grabbed her spiral and turned to a fresh page. "Why didn't I think of him?" she said. "He's cute. And smart. A little on the short side, but I can get over that," Tara added, marking an asterisk next to his name. "Going to Prom with Kobe wouldn't be so horrible."

"It's not Kobe," Jordan said, shaking her head as if she knew something that Nisha and Tara didn't. She paused for dramatic effect. "It's *Kevin* — from the baseball team."

"*Hot* Kevin? The pitcher?" Tara asked, quickly scribbling down his name. "Yes! No, wait. Isn't he going out with Carrie Logan?" She looked up from her notebook. "Forget it. I don't need any drama."

Nisha leaned across the table and whispered, "Well, I heard from Amy Bragg, who

49

heard it from Sonia Lewis, who happens to be Carrie's best friend, that Kevin and Carrie broke up three days ago. Apparently Carrie was devastated. . . ." Then she leaned back and shrugged. "But who cares? Carrie's a witch — and he probably dumped her because he likes you! Isn't that great?"

"Plus," Jordan added, adjusting the purple ribbon tied around her ponytail, "he was at the mall yesterday with Nate's crew, *and* Nate caught Kevin checking you out at a party once a few weeks ago. I didn't say anything to you because Kevin was still with Carrie. But now he's not, so . . ."

Tara smiled as she circled Kevin's name, her heart pounding. It definitely *sounded* as if he was the one. Tara could already visualize how awesome they'd look together, walking arm in arm into the Fairmont Hotel ballroom. Now, if she could only figure out what she'd be wearing.

"Uh-oh," Nisha said with a groan, causing Tara to pause her mini-fantasy about Kevin.

"What's up, Nisha?" she asked.

"Well, I just remembered another guy whose name starts with K," Nisha admitted. "The *other* Kevin. The creepy one."

Jordan wrinkled her nose. "Are you talking about that super senior with the scraggly goatee? The one who spends more time in the alcove with the metalheads than he does in class? Is he even graduating this year?"

"Don't know," Nisha replied in a serious tone. "But my friend Lauren from gym class says he's calling himself K-Dread now — ever since he got his hair twisted in Jamaica during spring break. What a weirdo."

"'Weirdo?' *Loser* is more like it." Tara refused to even write his name on her list. "I'll totally die if it's him," she added, covering her face with both hands. "It can't be him."

"It's not him," Jordan assured her . . . then paused. "Wait, doesn't he do garbage duty in the food court at the mall?"

Ewwww! It's him!" Tara cried, feeling suddenly nauseous and wishing that she'd said no to the chicken salad. "I can just feel it . . . and it's soooo slimy."

"Tara, I'm kidding!" Jordan said, laughing at the minor meltdown. "I never saw K-Dread cleaning the food court, I swear."

"And guess who I just caught glancing over here," Nisha sang, discreetly motioning with her eyes toward the jocks by the windows. "Kevin's sitting at Nate's table, and I saw him look at you a total of three times so far."

"Really?" Tara asked, dying to turn around but not daring to. But then she thought about it. Why *shouldn't* she look? Maybe it'd give Kevin the courage to stride right over to Tara's table and profess his undying love for her in front of her friends. Okay, maybe not that, but an alluring glance his way could, at the very least, send Kevin the message that she was interested.

As Nisha and Jordan began to chat about today's big game against Southside, Tara turned in the direction of the windows, determined to make eye contact with Kevin. But all she connected with was the cute spiky brown hair on top of his head, since he was focused on finding something in his backpack. Apparently he was in between admiring gazes at the moment. She'd give it a minute.

Hel-lo! Kevin! Over here! Tara thought after what felt like an eternity but was probably only about six seconds. *The object of your desire is staring at you. Aren't you going to take the opportunity to look back?*

Unfortunately the boy now seemed rather preoccupied with scratching something into his lunch table. Normally vandalism would be a turnoff to Tara, but she was willing to overlook the nasty habit due to Kevin's undeniable hotness. Tara listened to Nisha discuss Brian and the limo he was getting them for the prom, and Jordan mentioned a photography project that she was waiting to hear back on, but Tara was restless. She had only an idea about her admirer's identity but she still didn't know for sure. Kevin was right across the cafeteria! Should Tara just *sit* there and wait for him to come to her? What if he was shy? So shy that he might never get the nerve to approach her? How, then, would he ask her to the prom?

Like her father always said, "Nothing good comes to those who sit on their butts and wait." Determined to be proactive about the situation, Tara slid her chair back from the table and stood.

"Where are you going?" Jordan asked. "We've still got another fifteen minutes before the bell."

"I can't take the suspense anymore. I have to find out if Hot Kevin is my secret admirer or not," Tara replied with conviction, tossing her auburn curls.

Nisha's jaw dropped, her expression horrified. "Don't you think you might, um, *scare* him if you, like, *confront* him?"

"I'm not going to do that," Tara replied,

although the thought had crossed her mind. "I'm just going to, you know, pass by and see if he gives me a sign or something. Wish me luck!" With that she marched toward the windows, not knowing exactly how she planned to get Kevin to come clean about his possible crush. Whatever she did though, it had to be subtle, since he'd never respond to outright interrogation in front of his friends.

Plus, she'd promised Nisha that she wouldn't go that route.

"Hi, guys!" Tara said with a friendly wave when she arrived at the jock table.

"Hey, Tara. What's going on?" Nate replied.

A few of the other guys gave either the slight chin-lift hello or a casual raise of the eyebrows. Kevin, however, gave no reaction. In fact he barely acknowledged her presence as he continued to etch "Kevin wuz here" into the tabletop with what appeared to be his house key.

What is up *with that?* Tara wondered,

though she did marvel at how Kevin's sculpted right bicep flexed every time he pressed the key into his little project. If his arms were so cut, she could only imagine what his ripped abs looked like. . . . *No, stop it, Tara. You have to focus,* she reminded herself.

She tried to think of some clever way for Kevin to show a sign of devotion — *any sign* — when she noticed what he was having for lunch. Beside the hand that was so skillfully engraving his tag sat a double order of fries smothered with Velveeta.

Perfect!

Tara remembered the text that Kevin had sent yesterday and uttered it, word for word, since boys could be a bit dense at times. "Hi! Those fries look good. Can I have one?" she asked, deciding at the last moment to edit out the part about his being pretty. She reached for his plate.

Kevin surprised Tara by blocking her

hand midway. "Uh, I have a thing about fingers in my food," he said. "Sorry."

Feeling rejected, Tara quickly pulled back her hand. What did this mean? Did he miss the hint? Maybe Tara and her friends were wrong about the crush. Could that be it? Either way, Tara was beginning to feel like an idiot just standing there.

"Uh, you can have some of my Manwich, if you're hungry." The school mascot, Hector Something, who was in major need of a haircut, offered Tara his plate with a half-eaten sloppy joe sandwich on it. The entire table of jocks cracked up at Tara's expense.

"Ha, ha. Very funny," Tara spat, not at all amused and glaring at the boy who was now laughing with the rest of them. Tara resisted biting back with a mean comment, though it would have been very easy considering the unsightly unibrow the boy was sporting above his glasses. No wonder he was the class clown.

Instead, she chose to give Mr. Hottie

McSubtle one last shot. "I would have definitely shared my fries with *you*, Kevin, when I was eating some at the *mall*. . . . You know, *yesterday*?" she said, hoping that he'd finally get the hint this time.

But if Kevin did, he didn't show it.

CHAPTER *Five*

How can I do this without being obvious?
Jordan wondered as she grabbed her photography notebook and slammed her locker door closed, about to meet Nate to walk to their next classes together. After Tara's French fry test at lunch had proven inconclusive, Tara had assigned Jordan the task of probing Kevin's friend for information. Nate, of course, was the friend.

"Hey," Nate said, giving Jordan a quick kiss on the lips. "You ready?"

Jordan nodded and they began their usual trek down the crowded hallway. "So, I was wondering . . ." she began. "Does Kevin like anyone now that he and Carrie broke up?" She tried to sound casual as they pushed open the door to a stairwell.

Nate shrugged. "Don't know," he said. "Why?"

Crash and burn, Jordan thought. "No reason. Just wondering," she replied, feeling weird now for asking. Luckily she spotted three of her fellow cheerleaders, Ally, Brie, and C.J., heading down the stairs. They had their hair pulled into tight ponytails and were wearing the same white-and-purple uniform that Jordan was. She waved to them. "Ready to do those new cheers at the game today?" she called. Normally the squad didn't cheer for the baseball team, but they would this afternoon since the team was up against Emerson's archrival, Southside High.

"Hey, girlfriend," Brie said. "We are *so* ready."

"Yeah," C.J. added, nodding proudly. "Did you see the 'Student Newz' bulletin board outside of the principal's office today?"

"No." Jordan shook her head. "What's up?"

"You got, like, seventy nominations for prom queen when you only needed two," Ally said, grinning. "Congrats!"

"Are you kidding me?" Jordan asked, her eyes wide. She knew Tara and Nisha were going to nominate her, but she didn't think anybody else was going to bother.

"What about me?" Nate called down to the girls, who were now at the lower landing. "How many nominations did I get?"

Ally turned and shrugged as the three of them disappeared around the corner.

"Looks like I'm hanging out with royalty," Nate said to Jordan as they approached the second floor. "I hope after you win you're not going to make me bow when I pick you up for a date."

"Give me a break," Jordan groaned as she and Nate paused outside of her photography classroom. "You know I'm not like that. And how are you so sure that I'll win, anyway?"

61

"Oh, you'll win," Nate said, leaning against the wall. "Want to know why?" Jordan grinned and nodded as Nate pulled her close to him. "'Cause you're the most beautiful girl in the school," he whispered. "That's why."

Jordan knew it sounded cheesy, but she still liked to hear that Nate thought she was beautiful. "I'll bet you win, too," she murmured, wrapping her arms around his neck. Their first dance as king and queen of Emerson High played like a movie in her mind, with Jordan in her elegant white gown, and Nate wearing a classic black tux. To tell the truth, it didn't matter to her if they were voted royalty or not on that night, just as long as she was with Nate, dancing slowly in his embrace.

The late bell rang.

"Oops. Got to go," Nate said, back-shuffling down the hall. "See you later!"

Jordan's dreamy thoughts of prom night faded quickly as she slipped into the class-room under a disapproving glance from Mr.

Davidson. He was wearing his usual uniform of a loud Hawaiian button-down and a pair of bell-bottoms that looked as though they'd seen better days back in the thrift shop twenty years ago. She gulped and took her seat as he handed back each student's project portfolio.

The class was mostly filled with seniors who were looking to score an easy A during their last semester at Emerson. Jordan had started out with the same attitude, but soon realized that she liked taking pictures both digitally and the old-school way with film. Unbeknownst to her and the other students, Mr. Davidson's class turned out to be quite a challenge, but Jordan didn't mind. Mr. Davidson wasn't just a teacher. He was an artist who had work displayed in Chicago galleries several times a year.

Mr. Davidson approached and dropped Jordan's portfolio on her desk. "I expected more from you, Ms. Taylor," he said gruffly.

Huh? Jordan opened her portfolio and read the title sheet of her project: JORDAN

TAYLOR: AN INTROSPECTIVE. Underneath the title was her grade, written in red on a yellow Post-it note affixed to the page.

I got a D? Jordan thought as her stomach fell. *I've never gotten less than a B — how could I get a D?*

Mr. Davidson had written the dreaded "See me after class" underneath her grade, so she'd find out soon enough.

During the slideshow that ensued, Jordan kept comparing her own work to the projects that were considered *excellent*. She didn't get it. What was so special about Natalie Sigmond taking a picture of her face every day for a month? Why did that deserve an A? And, quite frankly, Charlie Bosworth's retrospective on his walk-in closet didn't seem all that enlightening to her.

Finally the bell rang, and Jordan waited until the other students had filed out of the room before approaching Mr. Davidson's desk. She knew exactly what she was going to say to him — that there must have been some mistake, that she'd worked really hard on this project and didn't deserve the poor grade. But as soon as Mr. Davidson glanced at her she crumbled, and all that came out was, "What did I do wrong?" and "How can I fix it?"

"Jordan, did you even think about this project at all?" Mr. Davison asked, leaning forward over his desk. He motioned for her to hand him her portfolio.

"Of course I did," Jordan replied, giving it over. She watched the teacher open it, trying not to stare at the top of his balding ponytailed head. "As a matter of fact, I think my pictures were a lot nicer than some of the other ones," she added firmly, sticking up for herself.

"Composition-wise your pictures were fine. But this project was an *exposition*," Mr. Davidson said, drawing out the word. "It's about getting to the core of your subject. In this case, *you*." He turned to the first page. It was a photo of Jordan's cheerleading squad celebrating at the regional competition last month. They'd been thrilled about coming in second since it was the first time Emerson High had ever placed in Nationals. And it had been a proud day for Jordan since she had led them there.

The teacher flipped through the other photos: a shot of a lone pom-pom on the floor in the gym . . . a close-up of Jordan and Ally, giving a thumbs-up to the camera.

"I know you're Emerson's little darling," Mr. Davidson added, "but there's got to be more to you than *this*. Right?" He pointed to Jordan's favorite of the sequence, a silhouette of Nate throwing a football into the sunset. "What you have here is all fluff, Jordan."

Ouch.

"But I'm a cheerleader," Jordan said softly. "It's my life." She hadn't planned it that way but that was how it had turned out, and cheerleading definitely had its merits. It had helped her score a free ride to Northwestern University in the fall, hadn't it? "What else am I supposed to do?" she asked, feeling the slight sting of tears behind her eyes. "Do you want something edgy? Is that it?" She willed herself not to lose it in front of her teacher.

"It's not about what I want." Mr. Davidson shook his head and flipped her portfolio closed. "It's about *digging deeper*. Show us your *truth*, man," he said, patting his chest with a fist.

Jordan nodded, afraid to even ask Mr. Davidson what he meant by any of that.

After school, as Jordan and Nate walked hand in hand toward their respective locker rooms to prepare for the big game against Southside, Jordan explained the net result of her conversation with her photography teacher. "Mr. Davidson said he's going to give me a chance to do the project over, but this time he wants to see the *real* Jordan Taylor . . . or else the D stands," she finished with a sigh.

"What a total idiot," Nate said, shaking his head. "It's almost the end of the school year. Doesn't he know that you've got other stuff to worry about — like the prom and graduation and going to college next fall? You don't have time for this."

Jordan was grateful that Nate was on her side, but now that she'd had a few periods to think about it, she could sort of see the teacher's point. "I think he's trying to get me to reveal something deeper about myself."

"Like what?" Nate said. "I mean, you're a cheerleader — a really hot one. What else is there to know?" He laughed a little too hard.

Jordan didn't think what Nate had said was so funny. As a matter of fact, she found it a bit . . . offensive. Maybe her looks made her prey to the whole blond cheerleader cliché, but she was far from stupid, and if anyone should know that it was Nate. "What do you mean?" she asked, pulling his hand so that he'd stop walking. "Don't you think I have any substance?"

"Sure, but come *on*, Jord," Nate said. "I mean, I'm an athlete and you're a cheerleader. Soon we'll be prom king and queen."

He scoffed. "That's who we are. What's wrong with that?"

Jordan shrugged and started walking again. "Nothing, I guess," she said, though something in the tone of Nate's voice bugged her. It was as if the mere idea of her having more going on in her head than pom-poms and popularity contests was ridiculous. Whatever. Maybe she was just being sensitive because Mr. Davidson didn't like her project. "Okay, well, have a good game, Nate," Jordan said, dropping his hand when she arrived at the girls' locker room. "See you out there." She gave him a quick kiss on the cheek, pulled open the door, and let it swing shut behind her.

"Hey, you guys. She's here!" a cheerleader named Tania called as soon as Jordan stepped inside the locker room.

"It's our prom queen!" C.J. leapt into Jordan's path, holding a feathery pink boa around her shoulders. She pulled it off with a flourish and wrapped it around Jordan. Then Ally stepped forward and fixed a plastic rhinestone tiara atop Jordan's head and rushed back to join the rest of the team, who all had their pom-poms set.

Brie shouted the call to the girls. "Ready, and —"

"Go, go, Jordan. Make us proud. We want a prom queen. Shout it out loud. Prom queen, prom queen, prom queen dream! Jor-dan! Jor-dan! Yaaaaaaaay, team!"

The cheerleaders whooped and hollered as they swarmed and hugged Jordan, congratulating her on the grand-slam prom queen nomination.

"You guys are so cheesy! I love it!" Jordan cried. But she was faking her enthusiasm. She knew she should be thrilled to have the support of her friends from the squad. It was such a sweet gesture.

But amid cheers of "Make us proud, baby!" and the "Whooooos!", all Jordan could hear were Mr. Davidson's words. *There's got to be more to you than this. Right?*

CHAPTER *Six*

Tara tapped her hands on the steering wheel of her mom's white Toyota Corolla as she sat parked at the end of Nisha's block. She was waiting for Nisha to sneak out of her house so they could go to Sam Sloane's party together. The thing was, Tara had been waiting for a full thirty minutes. She checked the digital clock in the dashboard. Make that thirty-*two* minutes.

Okay, now Tara was beginning to worry. *I hope Nisha didn't get caught*, she thought, resisting the urge to grab her handheld resting in the cup holder underneath the car radio and speed-dial Nisha's number.

Then, as if by mental telepathy, her phone chirped. Tara picked it up, relieved to find that Nisha had sent her a text message.

B there in 2

Moments later, Tara spotted a nervous-looking Nisha racing down the street in her black capri leggings and pink sleeveless tunic, a small leather clutch tucked under an arm and a pair of pink peekaboo heels dangling from her fingertips.

"Oh, my God. I thought your parents caught you," Tara gasped as Nisha opened the car door and slid into the passenger seat.

"Tell me about it," Nisha said, leaning back and breathing heavily from her recent sprint. "I don't know how my sister was able to sneak out when she was in high school. My father got up for some Tums the first time I tried to leave and I had to hide in the hall closet for twenty minutes." Nisha dropped her cute pumps onto the car floor and slipped her feet into them. "I swear I thought I was going to have a heart attack."

"Hey, at least you would have gone out looking gorgeous," Tara replied, glad that her parents never put the tight leash on her social life that Nisha's parents had on hers. She turned the key in the ignition and pulled the Toyota away from the curb.

Nisha laughed, seeming to relax a bit as she flipped down her visor and primped her long mane in the lighted mirror. The front and sides were pinned up on top while the rest fell into perfect curls down her back. "It almost seems like a waste of a good-hair night since Brian won't be at the party," she remarked. "He's babysitting his little cousin."

"You mean it's just us girls getting into trouble this evening?" Tara asked with a devious grin. It'd be nice to share a night of harmless flirting with guys with her girl-friends for a change. "Oh, and Nate," she added with a sigh. "Never mind."

Before Tara knew it, she and Nisha had squeezed the car into Sam's packed driveway, entered the party, and had sodas shoved into their hands by some random boy that Tara had never seen before and, by the amount of acne on the poor kid's face, didn't want to see again till he paid a visit to the dermatologist.

"I'll bet my prom date is here," Tara shouted optimistically to Nisha over the awesome cover band that was rocking out on a makeshift stage set up in Sam's living room. Holding their cups high, she and Nisha squeezed through a packed hallway that connected the kitchen, where the food and drinks were, to the main party area, where the dancing was. Tara had to admit she was feeling pretty good tonight despite the weird lunchroom incident with Kevin this afternoon. And, if she did say so herself, she was looking mighty cute in her green silk V-neck, khaki short-shorts, and a pair of strappy sandals.

She bopped her head to the beat as she scanned the crowded room of kids dancing and flirting. She noticed Nate and Jordan huddled in deep conversation in a corner, some girl with a black ponytail laughing like a hyena with Moose and that mascot kid, a few football players and cheerleaders setting up a game of some sort on the coffee table. . . . Then, Tara's eyes paused on Kobe Finnegan, who was sitting on the arm of a plaid couch talking to some guy she didn't recognize.

Not bad for a possible secret admirer, she thought, sizing up Kobe's clean buzz cut and the classic wire-rimmed frames he was wearing. Preppy-cute. How come Tara never noticed how adorable he was before? "There's Kobe," she said, leaning close to Nisha's ear so that Nisha could hear her over the music. "Think I should I go talk to him?"

The band launched into the classic Kelly Clarkson tune Since U Been Gone, and instead of answering Tara, Nisha screamed, "Oh, my God! I love this song!" She grabbed Tara's hand and the two of them pushed their way to the center of the dance floor to shake it.

A minute later Jordan was there, too, swinging her hair and her hips. She had her digital camera with her and held it out to snap picture after picture of the three of them, bouncing and singing the lyrics at the top of their lungs. "Where's Nate?" Tara asked, and Jordan surprised her by answering, "Who cares?"

Three songs later, the girls were still grooving and Tara felt herself relaxing and losing herself in the pulsating music. Kobe would just have to wait until the band took a break to get to know her.

Nisha leaned in and slung an arm around Tara's shoulders. "Looks like your secret admirer is staring at you," she said in a sing-song voice.

"Where?" Tara asked, turning. She expected to see Kobe by the couch but instead spotted Kevin, who happened to be wearing a pale blue T-shirt that contrasted with his spiky brown hair and olive skin in a way that made her shiver with excitement. Knowing that she looked totally great and feeling a rush of boldness, Tara smiled at Kevin.

And he smiled back!

So I was right. That whole thing at lunch was a front for his buddies, she mused. *Hot Kevin really* does *like me. This is good.*

Tara casually turned away from Kevin to dance with her friends. Pretending to ignore him, she raised her arms above her head and tossed her chocolate-brown curls, really getting into the song.

"He is so drooling over you right now," Jordan remarked a few minutes later, and Tara swiveled her hips to get his attention.

Sure it was a game, but Tara realized that she had to play it if she was going to get Kevin to ask her to the prom. She glanced over her shoulder to see if he was still interested.

Uh-huh.

By the time the song ended, Tara was confident enough to make her move.

"Go get him," Nisha said.

"Good luck, girl," Jordan added.

Shoulders back, head held high, Tara began her best *Top Model* strut across the dance floor in Kevin's direction. Maybe it was the intense way he was gazing at her, but Tara wasn't feeling the need for luck at the moment. She had a hunch that *someone* was about to snag herself a prom date — right now!

At last, a date I can be proud of! She resisted the urge to hop onto the nearest chair and shout it out to the whole senior class.

Kevin sat up and grinned at her again, then glanced away, seeming shy now, which Tara thought was so endearing. Heart soaring, she returned his grin while raising her right hand to offer a demure wave as she approached the moment of truth.

"Kevvvvvvvviiiiiin!" A brunette with a disheveled ponytail startled Tara as she unexpectedly stumbled past her, cutting off the path to Kevin. "I'm soooooosorrrryyy . . . It wasssallllmyyyfaulllllt," the girl blurted out.

Is that Carrie Logan? Tara wondered. *It can't be — not now! They broke up three days ago! Right?*

The girl tripped and fell into Kevin's lap, and less than a second later the two of them were kissing.

Which, much to Tara's dismay, answered her question — and then some.

CHAPTER *Seven*

"Miss Nisha, Miss Nisha will you help me with my *ghunghroos*?" six-year-old Anjani asked in the cramped and somewhat chaotic dressing room at the Todi Studio for Indian Classical Dance. She lifted her left leg and jiggled her bare foot for emphasis. "Please?"

"Of course, sweetie," Nisha said, and knelt down to tie a band of bronze bells around each of Anjani's tiny ankles. All around her, little girls wearing black leotards topped by *lahengas* in every color of the rainbow chatted excitedly as they adjusted their *ghunghroos* and jingled in and out of the dressing room before their lesson in the classical art of *Kathak* began.

Was I this cute when I first started dancing? Nisha wondered. She was in her own costume — a purple *lahenga* and matching *churidar* pajama pants — and as psyched as she always was on Saturday afternoons. It was the day she got to help her dance guru, Gargi Kumar, with the elementary *Kathak* classes.

Nisha had been studying *Kathak* for eleven years now and loved recounting Hindu mythological tales through movement. *Kathak* was like a language in itself; a sideways glance, a small twitch of the neck. . . . It all held great meaning, and the rhythmic movements were so beautiful to watch. Although she was considered one of the Todi Studio stars, Nisha knew that she still had a long way to go before her hand gestures, footwork, and spinning were even half as graceful as her teacher's. Speaking of which, Nisha didn't want the girls to keep the teacher waiting.

Nisha stood and clapped her hands for attention. "Come on, everybody. Time to move into the studio. We all want to be prepared when Guru begins class, don't we?" She felt like an Indian Pied Piper as she herded the little ones out of the dressing room and they jingled onto the hardwood floor of the studio across the hall. She had the girls form a horizontal line in front of a wall of mirrors. "Let's see if we can list the *navras* before Guru comes in," she told the girls. The *navras* were the nine expressions that *Kathak* dancers used to help act out a story.

With their backs upright and toes pointed outward in first position, the young students recited the *navras* in harmony, "Peace, heroism, anger, surprise, disgust, sympathy, comedy, fear, happiness."

"Excellent!" Nisha was praising them just as their guru made her entrance. Gargi Kumar, a slight yet regal woman with hair braided down the middle of her back, seemed to float on air as she skittered elegantly to the front of the room in a pale green sari, arms open wide.

Nisha and the girls placed their palms together in front of their chests and bowed their heads slightly to salute their teacher.

The guru returned the gesture and asked, "Are you ready to tell the fisherman's story?"

"Yes!" the girls cheered and stomped their feet, ankle bells chiming with the rhythm.

"Let's get started, then." Mrs. Kumar motioned for music, and the sitar player positioned in a corner near the windows began playing. The dance began with basic footwork to an eight-beat count. *"Ta, thei, thei, ta . . . Aa, thei, thei, ta . . ."* the guru chanted the tempo in time.

Nisha was watching their girls closely, gently correcting foot positions, when she noticed a tuft of blond hair through the tiny window in the studio door. She saw the hair ascend in the pane to include a forehead, a pair of eyebrows, and then two blue eyes that gazed into the studio.

Brian.

What's he doing here? Nisha wondered, her face flushing. She excused herself from the class for a moment and scurried to the door, bells jangling. She found Brian on the other side of it, his broad smile in full force.

"Sorry, I couldn't wait. I thought you might be done." Brian took her hands. "Whoa," he said, opening Nisha's arms and checking out her colorful garb.

Nisha found herself blushing — not because she was ashamed of her outfit, by any means. It was just that Brian was used to seeing her in typically trendy clothing: jeans, tanks, maybe a fitted blazer or wedge heels. He had never seen Nisha wearing as much as a silk scarf, let alone an entire outfit made of the fabric — complete with golden bangles on her wrists and *ghunghroos* on her ankles. She wondered what he thought of it all.

"You look . . . amazing!" Brian said.

"Really?" Nisha was thrilled that he was into it. "Thanks!" She showed off a quick heel-spin while positioning her hands to look like a budding lotus flower as her *ghunghroos* tinkled softly.

"Those bells on your feet are hot," Brian commented.

Nisha giggled. "I don't think the temple *Kathakas* back in 500 B.C.E. meant for them to be a turn-on," she said.

"Well, they are . . ." Brian murmured before going in for a kiss.

Nisha instinctively pulled back, checking left and right down the hallway, hoping that nobody had seen them. She desperately wanted to kiss her boyfriend, but she couldn't risk her guru or a parent of one of the students seeing them. The Selina Indian community was far from expansive, and getting caught making out in the Todi Studio for

Indian Classical Dance — with an American hottie, no less — would be cause for some major gossip. Gossip that would most certainly get back to Nisha's parents, which would, to say the least, be bad.

Still, Brian's luscious lips were right there in front of Nisha, calling to be kissed. . . .

"Follow me," Nisha whispered, taking Brian's hand and escaping into the students' changing room. Once inside with the door closed, Nisha slid her arms around Brian's neck, closed her eyes, and pressed her lips to his in a long, dreamy embrace.

When they parted, Brian leaned in again to give her an extra-sweet peck on the nose. Then he said, "I wanted to show you this." He tugged something from his jacket pocket and handed it to her. A catalog.

Nisha stared at the chiseled model on the cover who was squinting somewhere off into the distance, apparently feeling very manly, wearing an unbuttoned shirt and slinging a white tuxedo jacket over his right shoulder. Nisha stifled a laugh and hoped this wasn't the tux, or the mood, that Brian was going for.

"I picked this up at Tuxedo Depot in the mall," Brian explained. "The sales guy said that I'd be better off renting a tux now since the pickings get pretty slim once it's heavy into prom season." He took back the booklet, turned to page twenty-three, and pointed to a classic black tux with a cream-colored vest and a long cravat, as opposed to a bow tie. "I thought this one was good, but I wanted to see if you liked it." He flipped past a few more pages and pointed out a tux that had a white jacket and black pants. "This one's cool too . . . or this one," he added, pointing to a tux with tails on the opposite page.

Nisha smiled wide as a fuzzy warmth surged through her body. Brian had come all the way here just to show her a tuxedo catalog? This could only mean one thing. Brian, her sweet, laid-back Brian, was just as excited about the prom as she was!

And what an incredible night it would be. They'd probably start by exchanging flowers. Brian would get her a wrist corsage that matched the color of her dress, and Nisha would give him an understated boutonniere to pin to his lapel. Then they'd have that romantic ride in a stretch limousine to the Fairmont Hotel, and they'd tell the driver to take the long way around. An evening of fine dining with friends would be next, followed by luxurious dancing — so slow and close that Nisha and Brian would be able to count the beats of each other's hearts. Of course, the party would end when the night was still young. Who knew what would happen afterward?

"What?" Brian asked. "Why are you staring at me like that?"

"No reason," Nisha replied, her cheeks beginning to hurt from that goofy grin on her face. Feeling cuddly, she slid her arms inside her boyfriend's jacket and around his waist and rested her cheek on his chest. Nisha felt something solid on the inner pocket. "Hey, what's this?" she asked, digging inside it and pulling out a long black velvet box.

"Oh. Um, that." Brian turned crimson as he took back the box. "You weren't supposed to see it yet," he said, then paused. "But since you did . . ." He opened the box to reveal a silver bracelet with a heart-shaped charm on it. On the charm was an inscription, N+B.

Nisha gasped at the sight. "It's for me?" she whispered, knowing very well that it was and dying to try it on.

Brian nodded and removed the bracelet from its box. "I was going to give this to you on our date next Saturday," he said. "I wanted you to have something special for our six-month anniversary. Do you like it?"

Like it? Nisha gladly held out her right arm to accept the gift and her heart swelled as he fastened the silver around her wrist. Brian had to be the sweetest, most thoughtful, caring boyfriend ever!

"Oh, Brian, it's beautiful!" She held up her new bracelet and admired how the inscription twinkled underneath the lights. "I love it," she said, turning to Brian and drinking in his sparkling blue eyes. It was the closest Nisha had ever come to saying, "I love *you*." Nisha reached up to hug her unbelievable boyfriend.

"Anything for my girl," Brian whispered into her ear, then leaned in for another kiss.

Nisha's mind swirled as she pressed her lips to Brian's. She didn't hear the door to the dressing room open . . . until it was too late.

"Nisha!" Guru Kumar gasped at the sight of the entwined couple. "What are you two doing in here? Never mind. I *know* what you are doing!"

"Uh, maybe I should go." A very pale Brian exchanged a worried glance with Nisha, then slipped past Guru Kumar and out the dressing room door.

"Kissing a boy at the Todi? How could you shame your family like this?" The *Kathak* teacher's angry eyes demanded an answer.

"I . . . I can explain, Guru," Nisha stammered. "Just please, *please* don't tell my parents what you saw!"

CHAPTER *Eight*

"Guys . . . are total pond scum," Tara declared over the phone.

"Tell me about it." Jordan pressed the receiver to her ear, leaned her head over the side of her bed, and listened sympathetically to her friend vent about the Kevin-and-Carrie disaster last night. Thankfully, no one else had noticed the major flirt session that Tara and Kevin had going on only moments before he and Carrie had so "tastefully" gotten back together.

"Look on the bright side," Jordan offered, "at least you're not the rebound chick, right?" Jordan heard Tara heave a heavy sigh on the other end of the line. "Okay, how about this?" she added, wanting to make her friend feel better. "At least you didn't have to drive home a boyfriend who thought it'd be fun to challenge *Moose,* of all people, to a hot-wings-eating contest."

"Ew. I've witnessed Moose chow down an entire pizza with room to spare," Tara remarked. "Should I even inquire as to who won?"

"Is there *ever* a winner with those stupid boy tricks?" Jordan didn't bother waiting for an answer. "N-to-the-O," she said. "Nate got sick in the car, and I wound up taking a cab home from his house last night. I heard Moose didn't even make it out of Planet Wings before he tossed."

"Good thing you took Nate's ride to the party and not yours," Tara said.

"The only plus of the night," Jordan replied, thinking about how she hadn't really wanted to go to that party in the first place *or* to the fast-food after-show. "I'll tell you one thing, though. Nate *so* better make it up to me, and I'm not talking about buying me a tub of popcorn at the movies today," she added just as her call-waiting beeped. Jordan peeked at the screen on her phone and saw that it was Nate calling. "Hold on a minute, Tar. Guess who's on the other line?" She clicked the flash button and rolled onto her stomach. "Hi, Nate."

There was no answer at first, but then Jordan heard what sounded like a soft, painful moan. "Unghhhhhhh . . ."

He's still got a hot-wings hangover, Jordan thought. *Why am I not surprised?* "Uh, hel-*lo*?" she said into the receiver. Nate didn't respond right away, but Jordan had a good idea why he was calling — and it probably wasn't to ask what time he should pick her up for the movie.

"Jorrrddan?" Nate finally whispered. "I, uh . . . my stomach. It feels like a bomb exploded inside it. . . ." There was a long pause, and then, "I . . . I don't think I can . . . go to that movie today. Maybe tomorrow, okay?"

Jordan began to fume. She had known he was going to try and bail.

"Nate, today's the last day *Vert et Vrai* is playing," she reminded him. Why was it that whenever Jordan wanted to do something that was vaguely out of the ordinary, Nate had an excuse not to participate? Like back in January, when Jordan first started getting into photography and she'd invited him to go to a rare Alice Austen exhibit in Chicago. He'd suddenly developed plans to hit the indoor driving range with his buddies — only none of them played golf. She glanced at the time on the digital alarm clock on her nightstand. "Oh, and by the way, Nate. Thanks for calling me at the last minute to cancel."

"Sorry," Nate said. "I *would* go, but . . ."

"Whatever," Jordan replied. "Tara's on the other line. 'Bye." She hung up and pressed the flash button. "Tara?"

"What's up?" Tara said.

"How do you feel about seeing a French movie?" Jordan asked.

"The pond scum bailed, huh?" Tara replied.

"Big-time," Jordan said.

"I'd love to go with you," Tara told her, "but I can't. Jenny Brigger has summoned me to Starbucks in about thirty minutes for a *friendly* prom committee meeting, without the rest of the committee. She sounded almost nice about it. I think she wants to forge a truce. Maybe I'll offer her a crumb and let her handle the raffle at the prom-wear fashion show in a couple of weeks," she added. "We'll see how it goes. Sorry about the movie, girl. Buzz me later, okay?"

"Sure," Jordan said. Next, she dialed Nisha's cell phone to see if maybe she wanted to go to the movie with her, but then she remembered that Nisha had her dance class thing on Saturdays. She hung up before the voice mail came on.

"I guess I'm not doing much of anything today," Jordan muttered to herself, crossing the room and powering up the computer on the corner of her desk. As she slid into her chair and logged on to MySpace to see if anybody interesting was online, a tattered green flyer next to her keyboard caught her eye. It was the ad for *Vert et Vrai* that she'd picked up two weeks ago at The Lane, the landmark single-screen theater in downtown Selina.

Maybe I should take myself *to the movies.* She'd never gone to a film alone before. Would people think she was some kind of weird lonely girl without any friends? Jordan decided she didn't care. Once the lights went down, it probably wasn't much different than going with other people, anyway.

With no one to impress, Jordan barely swiped some gloss over her lips before leaving the house in her jeans, a long-sleeved tee, and her comfy old PRO-Keds. Twenty minutes later, Jordan was downtown and swinging into a parking spot near the old theater. She was psyched to see the long line of moviegoers snaking from the ticket booth and bending around the sidewalk, which to her indicated that the film must be pretty good. She took her place at the end of the line behind a dark-haired boy who was about her age and listening to an iPod.

Jordan opened her oversized leather tote and pulled out her mom's 35-millimeter, which she'd decided to take with her everywhere until she completed her photography project. She focused the lens and snapped a shot of the queue.

The boy in front of her turned and pulled out his white earbuds. "Nice machine," he said, gesturing to her camera. "Is that a Nikon F? I'd love to have me one of those."

"It's great," Jordan admitted. "I mean, digital is fine, but I find that sometimes you can't get the same effect you do with film, you know?"

"So, I take it you're into photography," the boy said, a warm smile spreading across his face. "That's cool. I'm Shane, by the way."

"Jordan," she said. Feeling friendly she added, "I take it you're into French movies."

"Hey, isn't everybody?" Shane said with a shrug, and grinned again. His dark eyes held her gaze for a moment before moving back to her camera.

"You want to take a look?" Jordan asked, holding it up. "I don't mind. Go for it."

"Thanks," Shane said as she handed it over.

As he examined her camera, Jordan surveyed the tall, lanky boy's uneven mod-cut hair, which was jet-black, and wondered if that was his real color or if it was dyed. Shane seemed cute in his slim black jeans and black hoodie, topped with a thrift-shop blazer. Not exactly her type, but he definitely had a style going.

He held the camera to his left eye, probably since a fringe of black hair was covering the right one, and focused the lens on Jordan. "This thing is solid," he said, lowering the camera and handing it back to her. "You're so lucky."

"I think I'd be luckier if this line started

going already," she replied, gazing ahead at some movement near the ticket booth. "What's up with that?"

Then one of the ushers emerged from the glass doors of the movie theater. "Sorry folks. *Vert et Vrai* is sold out. I repeat, *Vert et Vrai* is sold out. . . ."

"I can't believe this," she muttered, releasing a twinge of anger since it was Nate's fault that she hadn't come yesterday. Now she wouldn't get to see the movie at all!

"I knew I shouldn't have waited till the last day," Shane said as the line began to break up. He raked back the hair that was covering his right eye.

As he did this, Jordan found herself mesmerized by his fingertips. *Is that black nail polish he's wearing?* Upon closer inspection, she concluded that it was and forced herself to stop staring at it like the sheltered little suburbanite that she was. "I guess I'll get a Starbucks and head home," she told him.

"Starbucks?" Shane repeated with a pinched expression that that seemed to say,

Why? "I know a sweet café nearby. You can come with me if you want."

Jordan wasn't thrilled with the prospect of spending the rest of the day in front of the TV or on the Internet. *Why not?* she thought. The guy seemed harmless enough and kind of interesting. She was curious about what type of place he'd hang out in. "Where is it?" she asked him.

Shane pointed toward the corner of the bustling street. "It's just off Main, on Spruce."

The two of them weaved through the crowd on Main Street, then made a right onto Spruce Lane where they came across a nondescript storefront called Joes.

Upon entering, Jordan was greeted by a surprisingly funky decor. "Nice," she said, taking it all in. It was kind of rundown, but in a cool way. Tiny cracked black tiles made up the floor, and the exposed brick walls featured colorful works by various local artists, a few of whom, it seemed, were either lounging on the mix-and-match vintage couches or chatting with friends. A small stage graced a back corner, which Jordan assumed was used for open-mike nights. She liked the laid-back, do-your-own-thing vibe of the place.

She and Shane passed a pair of older gentlemen engrossed in a game of chess and made their way to the glass counter to order. Jordan selected some peach-mango chai, since the menu consisted entirely of loose teas, and Shane ordered an iced-tea latte mixed with beads of tapioca.

"How did you find this place?" Jordan asked, snagging a spot on a sectional near a pair of brightly painted French doors that were propped against a brick wall simply for art's sake. She took a cautious sip of her hot chai.

Shane shrugged and sat in a green wing-backed chair next to the couch. "I like to explore. One day I just walked in without knowing what it was." He nodded toward the bay window at a middle-aged man with a pencil-thin mustache having an animated conversation with a woman sporting a shock of orange hair and a ton of turquoise jewelry. "Those are the owners."

"Which one is Joe?" she asked.

"They both are," Shane replied. "But whatever you do, don't *ever* ask them which Joe the place is named after," he said, leaning in and lowering his voice. "Last year they had this huge blowout over the issue and closed down shop for a month," he added, taking a sip from the huge straw planted in his glass. "The only way they could resolve it was to get a new sign made . . . *minus* the apostrophe."

Jordan laughed. "They sound like a couple of characters," she said with a glance in their direction, noticing that they were now chatting up a brunette with a laptop who was near the door. "I like them already."

"They're good people," Shane said, "and they're always doing something to support the Selina arts community."

"I didn't even know Selina *had* an arts

community," Jordan admitted, feeling a bit sheltered again. "It's a nice surprise."

Shane tilted his head, his hair flopping over his right eye again. "Seriously?" he asked. "But you're a photographer — you're part of the arts community."

Jordan enjoyed the idea of that — even if she didn't *feel* quite so artsy in comparison to the others in the café. Come to think of it, she was enjoying her conversation with Shane, too. Usually she couldn't exchange ten words with a boy before he'd mention how pretty she was and that he'd like to take her out on a date sometime. Shane actually seemed to see her as a real person as opposed to some life-size version of Barbie. It was nice.

"I'm still learning about photography," she told him. "I'm carrying around this camera because I'm reshooting a project for school. My teacher says I need to work on capturing my inner soul, whatever that means. He thinks I identify a little too much with my inner cheerleader." She paused, reflecting on it. "I guess it's tough to separate from all that when your boyfriend is on the football *and* baseball teams, you know what I mean?"

"Uh, not quite," Shane said, and took another swig of tea from his straw.

Jordan wondered if she'd just caught a momentary flash of disappointment on Shane's face. Why, because she'd mentioned Nate? That was doubtful. She and Shane were so different, and Shane probably had a pale girlfriend with black hair and a lip ring around somewhere, anyway.

Shane put his drink on an old end table. "So you're a cheerleader, huh?" He seemed surprised. "I would have never guessed. You don't really give off that overly peppy vibe."

"Oh, I'm plenty peppy," Jordan said, oddly pleased that Shane saw a different side to her. "And it gets worse," she added, giving an exaggerated look over both her shoulders, then leaning in as if to tell him a secret, "I'll probably be voted *prom queen* in a few weeks," she whispered. "What do you think of *that*?"

Shane cracked up. "No wonder you need help finding an inner soul. You sold yours!"

"Oh, come on," Jordan said with a smile. "Being prom queen isn't *that* bad." She'd never had major feelings about it either way.

"But it *is*," Shane replied, his face growing solemn. "It's like reigning over something that represents everything that's superficial in today's society. I mean, maybe back in the day, the prom was pure, you know? Like, a simple dance in a gym or something. But now, it's turned into this huge frosty pink cake that all these industries are fighting to get a slice of: fashion, magazines, movies, hotels. . . . Prom is just one big consumerist vise of pressure and expectations and drama that's choking the innocence out of our generation." He bowed his head, shaking it. "Just, you know, for example."

Jordan raised her fingers to her lips, trying not to chuckle. This guy was so passionately *against* the prom. He was the polar opposite of Tara! "Does that mean you're not going to yours, emo boy?" Jordan teased.

Shane glanced up, his sallow cheeks slightly pink now. "You think I'm emo?" he asked with a wince.

Jordan grinned. "Maybe a little."

But she wouldn't hold it against him.

CHAPTER *Nine*

Random To-Dos

1) *No more daydreams re: Hot K.*
2) *Flirt w/Kobe (even though u r taller)*
3) *Start wearing kewl flats 2 skool*
4) *Tell Jordan 2 quit talking about nail-polish guy*
5) *Need deodorant, blush brush, new ringtone, microwave popcorn, and duct tape (4 Jenny Brigger's mouth!!!)*
6) *Find iPod*

"Hey, there's your boyfriend, Tara," Nisha said on Monday morning, abruptly interrupting her juicy story about getting caught with Brian to point out a scraggly K-Dread emerging from the third-floor boys' room in his gross black-leather motorcycle jacket.

Tara didn't know if it was because she'd skipped her grande mocha latte this morning, or if she was just in a sour mood, but she didn't appreciate the sarcasm. "Ha, ha," she replied, deadpan, as she, Nisha, and Jordan maneuvered through the crowded hallway en route to the AP English class that they had together. "Maybe you should save the matchmaking for someone else and just tell us what happened next, okay?"

"Yeah," Jordan chimed in, her eyes wide. "Is your dance teacher going to tell your parents? What's the deal?"

"My guru said that she wouldn't breathe a word . . . as long as I cut it off with Brian," Nisha went on, "so, I told her I would."

"Hold on," Jordan said, stopping midstride. "You said *what*?"

"It's not like she meant it." Tara took Nisha's right hand and displayed to Jordan the glittery silver charm bracelet on their friend's wrist. "It's really beautiful, Nisha," she commented.

Nisha brightened. "It is, right?" she said, examining the bracelet. "The only thing is, I have to be extra, *extra* careful now. That's going to be tough with the prom coming up."

"Or maybe you can actually try having a conversation with your parents," Jordan suggested. "Be straight with them. Who knows? They might understand. Aren't you tired of lying to them all the time?"

"It's annoying, but a girl's got to do what a girl's got to do," Nisha said with a shrug. "Believe me, my parents don't want to hear that I'm seeing someone. We've already had that argument. On several occasions. It all started around the time I got my first training bra."

"You're one to talk anyway, Jordan," Tara piped up. "You went on a date with Nail-polish Boy last weekend and didn't tell Nate about it. Isn't that sort of lying?"

Tara was joking . . . but not. Jordan must have mentioned Shane's name about a hundred times since Saturday. If Jordan and Nate's relationship wasn't so solid, Tara might have said that her best friend was dangerously close to having a crush.

"Puh-lease," Jordan said, rolling her eyes. "Shane and I are just friends . . . if that," she added as they started down the hall again. "I don't think I even know his last name."

"Just be careful," Tara offered. "Nate's a great guy. I wouldn't want to see you lose him over some non-friend."

"Have you talked to Nate yet?" Nisha asked.

"He's still in hiding," Jordan admitted, "so he has no idea that I've already forgiven him about the movie. Maybe if I milk it, he'll get me a pretty bracelet like yours."

The girls turned a corner, nearing Tara's locker. "Do you guys mind if I check if I left my iPod in here?" she asked. "I can't find it anywhere. It'll only take a second." As

Tara approached her locker, she noticed a folded piece of paper taped to the blue metal door . . . along with one long-stemmed red rose!

"*Tara!* Who's it from?" Nisha wanted to know.

So did Tara. "Wait a sec," she said, pulling the paper and the rose off the locker door and opening the folded note. Her fingers were trembling. "'Sorry we couldn't hang out at Sam's party. It was too weird. Meet me by the bleachers after practice today, okay? I really want to talk to you — K,'" she read aloud.

Tara handed the note over to Jordan's outstretched hand, and Jordan read it silently. "Okay, I'm officially confused," she said after she'd finished. "Didn't Kevin get back with Carrie?"

Tara nodded, replaying the awful scene in her head. "He was all over her at the party, which is probably why he felt weird," she admitted, wishing that it wasn't true. But it was, and Tara wasn't into being someone's second choice. . . .

"Excuse me, but you're *both* wrong," Nisha piped in. "Kevin didn't get back with Carrie, and he wasn't all over her at Sam's party on Friday. *Carrie* was all over *Kevin*," she added firmly. "There's a difference."

Was there? Tara wondered.

Tara was still contemplating this question after the end of eighth period. At first she'd come to the conclusion that, no, it didn't make a bit of difference who was all over whom. How would it look if she accepted a date with Kevin after he was seen making out with his ex only two days ago? No, she couldn't do it, simply on the principle of the matter. And Tara was nothing if not principled.

But then she thought about it some more. What would it be like if the situation was reversed? What if, say, Charlie Bosworth, however unlikely an example, stumbled over to Tara at a party, all emotional and upset, and proceeded to try to kiss her only moments before she and Kevin were about to connect? Tara would want Kevin to at least give her the courtesy of hearing her out.

And that's what I'm going to do, she decided. *Listen to what Kevin has to say and* then *make a decision. Just as soon as my prom committee meeting is over.*

Tara exhaled with a sense of relief that she hadn't felt for days. At least she had a solid plan for something — even if it *was* only for the next hour or two of her life. As she strode down the hall to dump her heavy advanced calculus textbook in her locker, she actually felt herself getting excited about the prom meeting. Surprisingly, she and Jenny had had a heart-to-heart over cappuccinos on Saturday and had come to an agreement on how to work together, considering their strong personalities. Tara had agreed to take Jenny's ideas more seriously, and Jenny had finally conceded that as prom chair, Tara did, in fact, have final say.

Tara threw the math book inside her locker, slammed the door shut, and saw Jenny heading her way. "Meeting time," Jenny called, tightening the pink scrunchie in her curly brown ponytail. "We've got prom committee stuff to do *pronto*."

Pronto? Jenny was still beyond annoying, but Tara resisted the urge to comment on it. In addition, Tara desperately wanted to tell Jenny that it *really* wasn't a good idea to wear a scrunchie — except maybe when you're washing your face — but she didn't think Jenny was the type to accept fashion advice gracefully, even if it was for her own good.

Tara and Jenny arrived at the basement classroom they used for prom meetings and were greeted by the two other members of the committee, who seemed to avert their gaze as soon as they saw Tara. *What's their problem?* she wondered, though not really caring. Unloading her stuff on a chair, she took her place at the wipe-off board.

"Okay, everybody, we have a lot to do and a little time to do it in," she said, choosing a red dry-marker from the holder underneath the board. "Everything is just about set for the upcoming prom-wear fashion show so now we can really focus on the prom itself." She pointed the marker at a boy with a mop of scruffy brown hair and an enormous pair of headphones clipped around his neck. "George, you're in charge of music. I'll need a list of six DJs plus their sample CDs and pricing. Think you can get it done by the end of the week?"

"I guess," George said, and scribbled something in his notebook.

Tara nodded and went on. "Stuart, please see about getting the tickets printed," she ordered a slight kid with sandy-blond hair. "Figure on getting a thousand. Show us the ticket design by Friday, too — nothing too crazy. You've got all the details except the price," she said. "I'll get back to you with that."

Finally Tara turned to Jenny, in ultimate Chair mode. "Jenny, can you arrange a meeting with the manager of the Fairmont sometime this week so that the two of us can check out the linen selections and pick the menu together?"

"What for?" Jenny replied snarkily. "Don't we want to get the theme settled before we go to the trouble of picking colors?"

Tara sagged her shoulders. *Again with the theme?* she thought, thankful that she'd held off on delegating the prom-wear fashion show raffle to Jenny at their meeting last Saturday. The girl clearly had issues with progress. "Come on, Jenny, we talked about this on Saturday. You agreed that the prom Chair has final say."

"I know what I said," Jenny replied coolly, her eyes fixed on Tara's, when the door to the classroom opened and Principal Harris entered the classroom.

"Okay, kids, I'm here," he announced with a smile. "What's this I hear about another dispute over the prom theme?" he asked, resting on the edge of the teacher's desk. "Talk to me, Tara."

Tara was confused, and a little rattled at the sight of her principal. "There's no dispute, Mr. Harris," she assured him. "We're going with my vision."

"You see what I mean, Mr. Harris?" Jenny turned to the principal, her face red. "She thinks she's the *only* one with a vision."

Now it was becoming clear to Tara. After their *supposed* friendly understanding on Saturday, Jenny had gone behind Tara's back and called in the principal. Again. Well, if Jenny wasn't about to play nice, neither was Tara. She turned to face the girl.

"Jenny," she said plainly. "I told you. Your 'Once Upon a Time' theme is tired. It's been done a million times before and it just isn't as cool as recreating Van Gogh's *Starry Night*."

"*I* think Jenny's idea is cool," Stuart Fullman almost whispered from his chair. "We can build this giant open picture book so that, like, people can take their prom photos in front of it and look like they're characters in a fairy tale."

Tara gaped at the boy. The idea was so cheesy. But it was also the most she'd heard shy Stuart speak in all four years of high school.

Soon tons of "Once Upon a Time" ideas were bouncing around the room.

Tara's jaw dropped, as she realized what was going on. *It's a mutiny,* she thought in horror. *A mutiny led by a humorless girl in a scrunchie.*

The prom is doomed.

"So it's settled," Mr. Harris said, seeming relieved. " 'Once Upon a Time' it is. I'm sorry, Tara, majority rules."

Tara's entire body was trembling. All that work she'd put into her *Starry Night* idea . . . and for what?

"I definitely think we should spend the rest of the meeting brainstorming 'Once Upon a Time.' We've already wasted enough time bickering over themes." Jenny turned to Tara with a pleased expression on her face. "Are you in or are you out? We sure could use you."

Wasted time is right! Tara wanted to storm right out of there and never look back, but *somebody* had to stop these people from turning the prom into a Disney-fest. "I'm in," she replied through clenched teeth. "But right now, I'm out. I've got to be somewhere."

She needed to seethe in private. Plus she had a secret admirer to meet.

Tara pulled her leather satchel onto a shoulder and left, trying to process what had just happened. Tara still thought that her idea was better, but if the prom theme had to be "Once Upon a Time" she was going to make sure it was the hottest "Once Upon a Time" prom Emerson High had ever seen.

And if she got to bring Jenny down in the process, even better.

She pushed open the double doors that led outside. Shielding her eyes from the sun, she crossed a large patch of grass, then walked along the edge of the orange track that was busy with kids leaping over hurdles and the cheerleading squad practicing their cheers.

Her stomach soured when she came upon

the bleachers and saw K-Dread and his loser buddies hanging out underneath the seating. *How come they're here and not by the alcove?* Tara wondered. She imagined for one appalling moment that *he* was the one who'd sent her the note. Thankfully, K-Dread did not so much as glance in her direction when she climbed the stands and took a strategic place in the top row. From that vantage point, she could view the track in front of her and the baseball field behind her.

Once settled, Tara watched a couple of boys leap over hurdles set up on the far end of the track. Then she focused her eyes on Jordan and the rest of the squad, who were in formation, ready to perform. Jordan shouted a call and led the cheerleaders in a final practice cheer. They were working with the mascot who, in full costume, performed a series of backflips in front of a pyramid that the girls had just formed. When he finished tumbling, he turned and waved excitedly to an imaginary crowd. *Not bad*, Tara thought. *Actually, pretty good.*

Soon she noticed that baseball practice was breaking up on the other field and spotted Kevin's spiky hair, olive skin, and broad shoulders right away. He and Nate were heading off the turf together.

It's now or never, Tara thought, doing a quick lip-gloss check and running her fingers through her curls before Kevin got there. Instead of crossing toward the bleachers, though, Kevin was following his teammates across the grass and into the school. *That's okay,* Tara thought. *He probably wants to take a quick shower before we hang out.* That was fine with her. Tara had no problem talking to a sweaty jock, but she drew the line when it came to smelly.

She leaned back and closed her eyes, enjoying the warmth of the sunshine while she waited for Kevin. She tried to push all thoughts of the awful prom meeting from her mind.

"Nice day, isn't it?" a boy said a few minutes later.

Tara knew without even opening her eyes that it wasn't Kevin's voice. Maybe if she pretended to be sleeping, the guy would go away. She didn't want to give Kevin any excuse to chicken out — and not wanting to bother her because she was talking to someone else could be considered one.

"Hey, Tara. Can I talk to you for a minute?" the boy added. He was certainly persistent.

Tara opened her eyes to see the mascot in his cougar costume standing at the bottom of the bleachers. "What's up?" she asked, not really caring to know.

"Uh, I, uh . . ." the boy said.

Why doesn't he take off that cougar head? she wondered.

"Spit it out," Tara told him, losing her patience.

"Uh, that calc quiz today sure was tough, wasn't it?" he said, setting a furry foot on the first row of benches.

"Not really. Math is my favorite subject," Tara replied curtly. She glanced around for

123

Kevin, hoping the mascot would get the hint and leave.

"Oh. Yeah, me too," the boy said. "Um . . ."

Tara sighed as the guy tried to formulate a complete sentence. This conversation was totally pointless. "Listen, I don't want to be rude or anything. . . ." she said, but couldn't help it. "I'm meeting someone here and it's probably best if I'm alone. You know what I mean?"

The boy removed his costume's cougar head, revealing his curly head. "Yeah, I know," he said, fixing his crooked glasses. "You're meeting *me* here. I'm the one who left the note on your locker."

Tara swallowed hard as she surveyed the mascot's serious face. He seemed so believable . . . but then she remembered what a prankster the kid was. He'd gotten a good laugh by offering her his Manwich at lunch the other day when she was trying to cop a fry from Kevin. He probably saw the note on her locker, read it, and thought it'd be downright hilarious if he showed up pretending to be her secret admirer.

"Very funny, Hector. You almost got me," she snapped, laughing. "You missed one thing, though. The guy I'm meeting has a name that starts with a K."

"Actually, Tara, my name's not Hector. It's *Victor*."

Whatever, Tara thought. *Just go, please.*

"*And* my last name is Kaminski," Victor added. "K-Man for short. All the guys on the athletic teams call me that. That's why I signed my notes *K*."

K-Man? Tara felt a chill run through her. First the prom meeting and now this? It wasn't Hot Kevin, or Kobe, or even K-Dread with the crush. She'd been wasting her precious time on those guys when it had been Hector or Victor or whatever his name was, all along?

Nooooo! Tara wanted to scream it at the top of her lungs, but she calmed herself. At least she still had four weeks to find a date to the prom. *It could happen.* She had to think positively. *The gods couldn't be any crueler to me than they have in the past day, right?*

She noticed Victor mustering the nerve to tell her something else. "So, um, I was wondering . . ." he began.

Tara's stomach lurched, knowing exactly what the boy was about to say.

No, don't do it, she urged silently. *Please. Do. Not. . . .*

"Would you like to go to the prom with me?" Victor asked, raising his unibrow hopefully.

He did it.

CHAPTER *Ten*

"If I go to the prom with Victor Kaminski, I'll be socially scarred for life!" Tara cried to Jordan and Nisha at lunch the next day.

"So does that mean you're going to the prom with him?" Jordan asked with a grin. Judging by the invisible daggers shooting from Tara's eyes, Jordan assumed the answer was no, which meant that Tara was back to square one. It turned out that Nisha had been wrong about Hot Kevin, and that he and Carrie had indeed gotten back together. And Kobe, although three inches shorter than Tara in flats, was a contender until Tara found out this morning that he couldn't —

and wouldn't — dance. So what was the point of going to the prom with him?

"Too bad we can't get the Fab Five to show up at Victor's house and magically transform him from geek to chic in a matter of thirty minutes like they do on that TV show," Nisha said, munching on a turkey sandwich.

"Please. I can do better than those guys with one credit card tied behind my back," Tara said with a dismissive wave of a hand, but then stopped mid-wave. "I *can* do better," she repeated almost to herself, and then looked from Nisha to Jordan. "Why don't I just *mold* Victor into an acceptable prom date?" she said, and Jordan saw her friend's face brighten. "I mean, I can't just sit around anymore, *hoping* for some cute guy to come to his senses and ask me. Prom will be here sooner than we think. Besides, how hard could it be to completely change someone's style and personality?"

"Oh, yeah. Piece of cake," Jordan said sarcastically. Nisha cracked up. Then Jordan

128

noticed that Tara was gathering her stuff. "You're leaving?"

"I've got to see if Victor still wants to go to the prom with me," Tara said, standing. "I might have been a little harsh when I rejected him yesterday."

After Tara marched down the aisle toward the jock table, Nisha turned to Jordan. "You know, I wasn't *serious* about the Victor makeover," she said.

"Yeah, but you know how Tara gets about a challenge," Jordan replied, finishing off the last bite of her burger. She knew that Tara had her work cut out for her, but Jordan herself had other things to worry about. Like what was she was going to show Mr. Davidson when he asked about her photography project next period.

She flipped though a bunch of old photographs, none of which seemed right. Then there was the picture of the line at the movie theater and one of some cottony clouds that she'd developed in the lab yesterday, but those didn't reveal anything personal about Jordan.

She examined the next photo. It was of Shane — the day they'd hung out at Joes. With elbows resting on his knees, fingers laced underneath his chin, Shane's intense gaze seemed to reach right through her. Jordan still had no idea what he'd been thinking about when she'd taken the picture.

"Ooh. Is that Nail-polish Boy?" Nisha asked, grabbing it from Jordan. "You didn't tell us he was so cute!"

Jordan shrugged. "Really?" she asked casually, though she didn't see how it was anybody's business how attractive Shane was.

"Oh, my God. I have the most awesome idea!" Nisha cried, doing her signature happy bounce in her seat. "Why don't you ask Shane if *he'd* go to the prom with Tara? That way she won't have to give her prom date a makeover. Well, except for the nail polish. He'd be willing to take it off for one night, right?"

"How would I know?" Jordan asked sharply. "Anyway, I don't think he's the type to do a prom." She wasn't quite sure why she was feeling so annoyed with Nisha for mentioning it.

"Oh, well. It was an idea," Nisha said just as a loud "YEAH, BABY!" rang out over the din of the lunchroom.

Jordan and Nisha looked across the room to see Tara and an extremely excited Victor. Much to Tara's obvious horror, Victor had leapt on top of the lunch table, Tom Cruise–style.

"Looks like Victor said yes," Nisha observed.

"I can't tell if Tara is relieved or repulsed," Jordan commented. *Maybe I* should *ask Shane if he'd take Tara*, she added silently to herself. He'd probably say no, but it couldn't hurt to try.

The bell rang.

"Hey, don't forget to cover for me tonight," Nisha reminded Jordan as she rose to her feet. "Brian's parents invited me over for dinner."

"Good luck," Jordan said, knowing it was Nisha's first time meeting them.

She met Nate by the lunchroom doors as usual, and he walked her to her next class.

"Are we going to Antonio's after practice today?" Nate asked when they reached her classroom.

It's always wings or pizza . . . pizza or wings, Jordan thought. She had a better idea. "Why don't we try somewhere different for a change?" she suggested. "I know this cool teahouse downtown."

"Can I get a Coke and a slice there?" Nate asked. "You know how hungry I am after practice."

"No," Jordan admitted. "But you can get a raisin scone and strawberry-mango chai. What do you say? Should we go?"

Nate laughed as if Jordan had said something amusing. "You're hilarious," he said, then left her with a peck on the cheek. "Later, babe."

Nate thinks I'm joking, Jordan realized. *When did he lose his sense of adventure? Not even adventure — all I asked was for him to try an after-school snack that wasn't pizza or garlic knots.* She sighed and turned to go into class, trying to think of something good to tell Mr. Davidson regarding her lack of photographical progress. When her cell phone rang, Jordan jumped. *Oops. I must have forgotten to turn it off when I got to school.* She checked the number calling her but didn't recognize it. Then she flipped open the phone. "Hello?"

"Hey, it's Shane."

Jordan smiled when she heard Shane's deep voice. After hanging out at the café on Saturday, she and Shane had agreed to keep in touch by exchanging numbers, though she never expected him to actually call.

"So I was thinking that maybe you might be interested in taking a little road trip with me after school," he said. "I found a theater in Eggersville that's playing *Vert et Vrai*."

"Really?" Jordan asked, excited. She was definitely willing to skip cheerleading practice for the movie. And Nate would be so busy with his buddies at Antonio's that he'd hardly miss her if she didn't go. "I am so there!" she cried.

Vert et Vrai. She'd get to see it, at last!

"What now?" Jordan asked Shane as they cut out of the movie early and emerged onto the sidewalk in front of the Eggersville Theater.

"We're on a mission," Shane said in a mock-serious tone. "To get out the bad taste that movie left in my mouth," he added, looking around.

"Popcorn?" Jordan offered him some from the enormous tub she was holding. "It's pretty good," she added, which, unfortunately, was more than she could say for *Vert et Vrai*.

Shane took a handful of kernels and nodded toward what looked like a park across the street. "Let's check it out," he said, and led Jordan past an enormous fish fountain by the entrance.

"Okay."

The small, quiet park consisted of a rectangular patch of grass surrounded by a wide, pebbled path with several empty bistro seats on it. Jordan guessed it was the kind of place people came on their lunch hour during work.

"I still can't get over how patronizing it all was," Shane sighed, stretching out on the grass, hands behind his head.

"Really," Jordan agreed, sitting cross-legged next to him. "At first I kept thinking it was going to get better, but after the first hour I was like, 'Hel-*lo*? I *get* it. You don't have to keep slapping me in the face with the symbolism!' I mean, come on, I'm not *stupid*."

Shane rolled onto his side to face Jordan with an amused expression. "I wouldn't describe you as stupid, Jordan. Actually, the word I'd use to describe you is . . . intriguing. Yeah. Definitely intriguing."

Jordan lips curled into a smile. "I like

that," she said, and pondered the words she'd use to describe Shane. Dark? Complicated? Soulful? She wasn't sure yet.

Feeling his eyes still on her, Jordan picked at a few blades of grass. She wanted to ask Shane something but was embarrassed by the question. It had to do with what he'd mentioned about her the first time they'd met. She took a deep breath and went for it anyway.

"Shane?" she began. "Do you really think I'm selling my soul to be prom queen?" It was probably just a joke, but for some reason Jordan cared what he thought about her. She chewed on her bottom lip as she waited for the answer.

Shane smiled slightly, then shook his head. "Nah, but if you've got to do some introspection for your photography, you won't find the truth in the rhinestones of some fake crown . . . or by screaming your heart out on the sidelines of a football field," he added, "but I think you've already got that one figured out."

"Maybe," Jordan said, hardly able to process her thoughts. *How could a boy who is so different from me — a boy that I just met — understand me so well?* Rather than try to figure it out, she leaned back into the fragrant grass, letting the early evening sun warm her face. "It's so nice out," she breathed. "I wish we didn't have to go home soon."

"We can chill here some more," Shane suggested, "or, if you're into it, I've got friends in a punk band called the Violent Kittens. They're playing the early set at a club in Chicago. You want to go?"

"All the way to Chicago?" Jordan asked, sitting up. "Are you serious?" The idea was exciting, but she wasn't sure she should do it.

Shane shrugged. "We're already halfway there."

Jordan considered it. Aside from the fact that she'd never seen a punk band play live, she'd never done anything so majorly impulsive before. "Well, since you put it *that* way," she said, a little thrill fluttering her stomach.

"Cool." Shane made a quick call home on his cell phone to inform his parents of the plan. Jordan was about to do the same when she noticed that Nate had called her twice and her mom three times. She'd muted her phone's ringer in the movie theater and had missed their calls.

Uh-oh. She paused her thumb over her contacts list as she checked the time: 7:15. *Mom's definitely pissed,* she knew. *And would she really let me go see a band play in Chicago on a Monday night anyway, even if I did call?*

"You ready?" Shane asked, standing and offering her a helping hand.

Jordan stared at the five missed calls on her phone. *I'm already in deep,* she thought. *Might as well go all the way.*

CHAPTER *Eleven*

To: *Bmoreschroder@quickmail.com*
From: *NishaK@quickmail.com*
Re: Dinner

Hi, B!

Have 2 buy something in shopping plaza by my house b4 dinner. Can u pick me up in front of Wegmans in 20 min instead of @ my house?
Love,
Nisha

"Who is this B?" Nisha's mother asked just as Nisha clicked SEND to shoot the e-mail to her boyfriend.

139

"Mom, hi!" Nisha immediately closed the window she was working in on her computer. "You totally scared me," she said, twisting in her desk chair to face her mother and putting a hand to her chest. "How long have you been standing there?"

"Just a few seconds," her mother replied, adjusting her fuchsia silk scarf across her shoulders. "Who is this B?" she asked again. "I thought you were going to Jordan's for dinner."

"I am," Nisha said casually, although slightly panicking as she tried to think of a quick fib that her mom would buy. "B *is* Jordan, Mom. She, uh, likes to go by her middle name, *Beth*, when she's online. You know, to fool the identity thieves or whatever. She's been kind of paranoid ever since she saw that exposé on *Primetime*," she added, hoping that wasn't laying it on too thick.

"Oh, that is a problem," Mrs. Khubani said, nodding. "That's why your father pays the bills the old-fashioned way. The computer can be more trouble than it's worth sometimes."

"Uh-huh." Nisha released a breath she didn't realize she'd been holding. *That could have gotten ugly,* she thought, relieved that it hadn't. Nisha shut down her iMac and tried to imagine what it would be like to come clean right now to her mom — to tell her the truth about Brian. She wanted to. But then she pictured the argument. The crying. The door slamming. The silent treatment and disapproving looks from the family until Nisha finally relented and broke up with her boyfriend forever.

Her parents would probably never trust her again. Would they still let her attend Emory University in the fall, or would they make her go to some nearby college so they could keep an eye on her? Worse yet, would they send her to live with family and study in India, where she would surely never see Brian again?

Why can't they just be like other parents? Nisha demanded silently, fuming. *Just for once? It's so frustrating!*

"Don't forget to tell your father and I when it is," Nisha's mother said, breaking into Nisha's thoughts.

"Huh?" Nisha had no clue what her mother was talking about.

"I asked you when the Todi Studio recital was," Mrs. Khubani said slowly, searching her daughter's face carefully. Then she sat on Nisha's white embroidered bedspread and patted the space next to her so that Nisha would sit too. "*Beta*, you've been so distracted lately. I am worried. Are you having trouble with your classes this term? Is that why you need to study at Jordan's house so much? Or is it because you're afraid about leaving us for college in the fall? Talk to me, *Beta*. I cannot help you without knowing what is wrong."

Her mother seemed so concerned that Nisha found herself wanting to tell her. *I'm in love, Mom,* she thought. *I'm in love and I can't share it with you. That's what's wrong.* If only she could say it out loud.

"It's nothing," Nisha replied instead. "Just that I found out that the prom is a formal thing, and I've got nothing to wear."

"Is that all?" Mrs. Khubani asked, appearing relieved. "I just bought some beautiful silk last week that would make a lovely sari."

Nisha rolled her eyes. After all these years her mother still didn't get it. "Mom, we're in *America*. I'm not wearing a sari to the prom; I'll look like a freak. It's bad enough that I'll be the only one there who isn't allowed to have a date because her parents are so strict!"

Nisha knew that she added the last part for the sole purpose of making her mother feel guilty, but now she wished that she could take it back. *I'm so stupid,* she thought. *Now Mom knows that there's dating involved.* Her mother opened her mouth to speak, but Nisha cut her off before she could say a word. "Oh, look at the time. I've got to get going.

I'll be home by nine." She quickly picked up her backpack from the floor next to her desk. "See ya!"

As she walked to the Wegmans shopping plaza, Nisha could only hope that she hadn't opened a can of worms by mentioning the dating. She wished her mother would forget about it. When Nisha arrived, she had just enough time to buy a pretty bouquet of roses for Mrs. Schroder at the florist before Brian picked her up.

"My parents are so psyched to meet you," Brian said when Nisha slid into the Civic.

"I'm a little nervous," Nisha admitted, clutching the flowers as they drove to his house. "I hope they like me."

Nisha relaxed as soon as Brian's mom opened the front door. "Nisha, finally!" Mrs. Schroder said, her blue eyes beaming. "We've been asking Brian to invite you over for weeks."

Nisha smiled and handed her the bouquet. "It's nice to meet you," she said softly.

Then she met Brian's father and his twelve-year-old sister, Sarah, who looked like a girl version of Brian.

"Brian's told us so much about you, Nisha," Mrs. Schroder said as they sat down for dinner.

"All good things, I hope," Nisha said, feeling more and more at ease.

They talked about everything from Nisha's dancing to Brian's lead in the school play last term to the upcoming prom. Nisha loved how the conversation flowed so easily in the Schroder household and how Brian and his sister gently teased each other. Then Mrs. Schroder disappeared for a few minutes during dessert, only to return with a large photo album.

"*Mom*, come on," Brian groaned. "Put that away."

"Why?" she asked, clutching the book to her chest. "I can show Nisha a few pictures if I want to . . . and I want to. Do you want to see them, Nisha?"

Nisha sat up in her seat and glanced at Brian, whose cheeks had turned bright pink. "Yes, please!" she said.

Mrs. Schroder sat in a chair next to Nisha, opened the album, and pointed to a picture of an infant in a pink jumper cuddled up in a blanket of the same color.

"Is that Sarah?" Nisha asked.

"Nope, that's baby Bri-bri," his mom said, cooing. "Look how cute he was."

"Mom!" Brian hid his face in a hand, and Sarah began to laugh. "You realize I'm going to need years of therapy after this humiliation," he added.

"They thought Brian was going to be a girl but got a major surprise when he was born," Sarah explained. "So Brian had to wear *pink* for the first six months of his life." She snickered.

"Oh, you're loving this, aren't you?" Brian said to Sarah, who nodded enthusiastically.

"Well, I think little *Bri-bri* was adorable," Nisha said, patting Brian's arm and giggling.

Mrs. Schroder flipped though the entire album, showing Nisha all the milestones in Brian's life: kindergarten, Little League, school plays, junior high, and high school photos. "And on this page," she said, turning to a blank spread, "is where I'll scrapbook your prom pictures." She turned to Brian. "Make sure you tell the limo driver to stop back at the house after you pick up Nisha. I want to get some shots of the two of you all dressed up. Is that okay with you, Nisha?"

"Totally," Nisha said. She liked Brian's family and the way they were so relaxed and casual around one another. Sometimes Nisha felt close with her own parents like this . . . and other times she felt like an alien in their home.

Before Nisha knew it, it was time to leave and Brian's mom was walking them to the door. "You should come by more often. We'd love to have you," Mrs. Schroder told Nisha. Just as Nisha and Brian were heading out the door she added, "Tell me, Nisha, what do your parents think of Brian? Do they like him as much as we like you?"

"Oh, they haven't met him yet," Nisha said hurriedly, and noticed that Brian's mom seemed surprised. "But they will soon," she added. "Maybe this weekend."

It was an easy enough lie, she'd thought.

Until the drive home.

Brian turned to her and said, "So, I'm finally going to meet your parents this weekend. . . . It should be good, right?"

He looked so nervous and excited. How on earth was Nisha supposed to tell him that she didn't mean it — that she didn't know if Brian would *ever* meet her parents?

CHAPTER *Twelve*

"*What* did you say?" Jordan shouted over the
thrashing guitars of the band onstage. A girl
with what looked like a tiny bone through
her septum, wearing a black tank and tartan
miniskirt, complete with ripped fishnets and
knee-high combat boots, pushed past her to
get closer to the stage.

"I said . . . are you *okay*?" Shane yelled in
her ear as the crowed bumped them from all
angles.

"Fine!" Jordan cried, though she knew
why Shane had asked. Glancing at her own
outfit of a pink sweater set, white cotton

capris, and the oversized vintage jacket Shane had loaned her to edge up her look — she knew she came off more like she belonged in an ad for J.Crew rather than in a grungy lounge. She definitely didn't fit in with the scene. For one thing, she'd showered this morning. For another, she was the only girl without at least one piercing on her face.

Shane, on the other hand, wore a rocking black-jeans-and-black-T-shirt outfit that seemed to work among the general public as well as with the punks — despite his good hygiene practices.

Maybe I should learn to wear black, Jordan thought, pulling out the elastic from her ponytail and messing up her 'do. She nodded her head to the beat of the music and watched the band play on the shabby little stage, not more than five feet from where they were standing. The lead singer, who wore her short, wine-colored bob in tiny ponytails all around her head, belted out a song as she strummed hard and fast on her electric guitar.

It's definitely different, Jordan thought as the speed of the music pulsed through her, though she couldn't decide if she liked it or not. Normally she was a strictly pop-and-maybe-a-little-reggae kind of girl, but soon she found herself dancing — okay, not really dancing, but jumping — alongside of Shane.

She raised one fist up and pulsed it toward the stage, whooping and bouncing along with the rest of the crowd. Shane slung an arm around her shoulders and did the same.

People were colliding into one another, but the mob was so into the band that no one seemed to mind. Moving to the music, Jordan held out her camera and snapped pictures of the crowd and the Violent Kittens. Then Shane grabbed the camera away from Jordan and photographed her going crazy on the dance floor. She didn't care that she probably looked like a maniac. It felt awesome and fun and liberating to go wild, letting the music take her to a place she'd never been before.

Finally the Violent Kittens strummed their last chord and the crowd was still begging for more. "You want one more?" the lead singer shouted in her husky voice, pointing her index finger toward the spectators. "Should we play another?"

Jordan yelled, "Yeah!" along with Shane and the rest of the room.

"Well, you're in for a treat," the singer said. "We've got an old friend in the audience — Shane Dresden. Some of you might not know this, but Shane here used to sing with VK when we first started."

Jordan's jaw dropped. She looked at Shane, who gave a shy smile and shrugged, indicating that it was true.

"Let's get him up here for a reunion!" the lead Kitten cried.

As the crowd shouted for Shane, Jordan pushed him toward the stage. Shane gave the singer a kiss on the cheek, then whispered something to the rest of the band. He took the microphone and said, "This is a *tender* song I wrote a while back. . . ."

Jordan felt a rush when Shane smiled and nodded to her right before he began the song. Surveying the crowd, she noticed a few girls looking her way, probably trying to figure out who she was. *Cool*, Jordan thought. It was the first time Jordan could say she was with the band and mean it.

"One, two, three, four!" The band launched into a clamor of speed metal as Shane growled lyrics into the mike.

"*This is a love song! Yeah, a love song! A freakin' love song! You. Broke my . . . hearrrrrrrt!*"

Jordan and the rest of the room went crazy, bouncing to the thump of the supersonic drums as Shane yelled out the song. When the instrumental came on, Shane leapt off-stage to dance with Jordan. A few minutes later, he was back onstage to finish it.

"*This. Love. Song. Suuuuuucksssss!*" he cried as he grabbed the microphone stand with both hands. Then he paused, catching his breath and staring out at the crowd. A tension in the air told Jordan that the song wasn't over yet. Finally Shane picked out a skinny brunette in the front and pointed to her. "And so . . . do . . . you," he said calmly.

The lead Kitten wound down the song with an impressive solo, then the band ended the tune with a final chord. The audience whooped and hollered as Shane hopped off the stage to join Jordan, who was by now exhausted and sweaty from dancing so hard.

"You're amazing!" Jordan cried truthfully, giving him a friendly pat on the back. "How come you don't sing with a band anymore?"

Shane shrugged, catching his breath. "My parents moved, so I couldn't drive an hour each way for practice — and once I got to Selina I figured out that the whole being-in-a-band scene wasn't my thing anyway. Which reminds me . . ." He glanced at his

154

watch. "It's getting kind of late. We should probably head back home."

Jordan nodded. "Okay. I'll meet you up front in a few." She pivoted and made her way down a narrow hall and into the ladies' room, which luckily for her did not have an enormous line snaking out of it. Jordan was surprised by the black walls covered with graffiti and old beer labels stuck to the mirror. *What did you expect, a puffy pink powder room?* Jordan approached the sink and splashed some water on her hot face when the ladies' room door swung open.

The lead singer for the Violent Kittens strode in, wearing her platform boots. Although she was much smaller than she seemed onstage, Jordan found herself a bit starstruck. "You were great out there," she told the girl.

"Thanks," the singer replied, leaning on a wall by a paper towel dispenser. She pulled one out and handed it to Jordan. "So I guess you and Shane are friends now, huh?"

Jordan nodded as she blotted her face

dry. "You could say that. We're good friends."

"Well, there's something I think you should know about your *good friend*, Shane," the girl said.

The tone of her voice told Jordan that the lead Kitten wasn't about to say anything nice. Jordan was interested despite the girl's obvious bitterness. Even though she and Shane had taken a fun road trip to Chicago together, Jordan still didn't know him that well.

"Let's just say that Shane's got a short attention span . . . if you know what I mean." The lead Kitten stepped closer to Jordan, her heavily shadowed lids magnifying the intensity of her eyes. "I'm telling you, get out before it's too late."

She thinks we're dating? At first Jordan wanted to laugh, but then she found herself getting . . . angry. What right did this girl have to come in here and tell Jordan what to do? By the looks of things, Shane probably broke up with *her*, and now Miss

Kitty couldn't bear to see him happy with someone else. *She sure is going to feel stupid when she finds out that Shane and I aren't a couple*, Jordan thought. "You don't have to worry about me," she told the girl icily. "Shane and I are friends. Only friends. That's it."

"Uh-huh. Right," the girl said. "Is that why you're wearing his jacket when it's two hundred degrees in here?" The girl peeled herself from the wall. "Don't say I didn't warn you," she added, then exited.

Jordan stared at the closing door. Ridiculous. Why was it so hard to believe that a guy and a girl could actually be friends? Yes, Jordan thought Shane was kind of cute in a weird way. That didn't mean that she'd ever date him though, did it? Whatever. Why was she even thinking about this?

Deciding *not* to anymore, Jordan threw her paper towel in the trash can and found Shane outside the club, leaning on his blue Mustang, waiting for her. Neither of them said much as they got into the car.

Against her will, Jordan dozed off on the ride home only to awake just as Shane was quietly pulling up in front of Jordan's house.

Shane put the car in park and turned to her. "Thanks, Jordan," he said. "For coming with me."

"I'm glad you called," she replied. "I don't think I've ever been this spontaneous before."

"Me neither," Shane admitted with a small smile.

"Really?" Jordan asked. "You seem like the type of guy that does stuff like this every day."

"Nah." Shane shook his head. "I knew how disappointed you were about not seeing *Vert et Vrai* and I guess I wanted to take you to see it. Too bad it sucked. I hope the band made up for it, though."

Jordan was stunned. "You mean, the road trip was all for *me*?" she asked. That was one of the nicest things anybody had ever done for her. Even Jordan's own boyfriend, although never stingy with sweet gestures, such as buying her granola bars on the way to school or leaving cute notes in her locker just to say that he was thinking about her, would *never* concoct a surprise plan to whisk Jordan away to see a foreign film.

"Thank you, Shane!" On impulse, Jordan quickly leaned in and wrapped her arms around Shane, who seemed startled at first, but then relaxed and hugged her back.

"Yeah, well . . ." Shane said, still holding her.

"Oh, I have something funny to tell you." Jordan pulled away so that she could see his face. "Your friend, the lead singer from the Violent Kittens, thinks that we're going out. Isn't that crazy?"

Shane nodded. "It's the stupidest thing I've ever heard," he said as he lightly brushed Jordan's cheek with his fingertips, leaving behind a ripple of pleasurable tingles down her face and neck.

Jordan suddenly felt nervous and warm

as she enjoyed the feeling of his hand, aware of a strange and exciting energy growing between them. It was as if their friendship had shifted into something else with one gentle touch. Was he feeling it, too?

She turned her gaze away from Shane and fixed it on the dashboard, too afraid to look at him.

"What's up?" Shane removed his right hand from her cheek and now leaned against the armrest that separated them.

Jordan observed his graceful fingers — artist's hands — maybe a piano player. Not rugged like Nate's — the kind she'd always thought she preferred. Finally, she found the courage to look into Shane's face and noticed for the first time that Shane had a tiny freckle underneath his dark, brooding left eye. She reached out and swept back his hair to see if he had one underneath his other eye. He didn't.

"I'm so glad I met you," Jordan found herself whispering as her gaze moved to study Shane's distinctive nose, his angular jaw, his soft pink lips, which were now curving into a faint smile. Inside her head she was reminding herself that she and Shane were supposed to be friends, but her body wasn't listening.

Jordan knew that she should pull away as Shane drew closer, his full lips only inches from hers, but she couldn't. Or more precisely, she didn't want to.

But I have to, Jordan told herself. *I have a boyfriend. Nate. He doesn't deserve this.* She turned her head away and leaned back in her seat. "Maybe I should go inside," she said.

"Yeah. Okay," Shane replied, clearing his throat.

Feeling clumsy and awkward, Jordan fumbled with the car door until she finally got it open and climbed out. *I almost kissed Shane*, she said to herself. *I can't believe I almost kissed him. . . . I can't believe I almost cheated on my boyfriend. . . .*

Abruptly she remembered what Nisha had suggested earlier — about asking Shane to attend the Emerson High prom with

Tara. *Maybe I won't feel so awful about what almost happened if I set them up,* Jordan reasoned.

She turned back to the car and bent down, leaning her hands on the open window of the Mustang. "Um, Shane, I was wondering. Would you like to go to the prom with . . . my friend Tara?" she asked.

Shane shook his head. "Thanks, but no thanks," he replied, avoiding eye contact by staring out the windshield. "Like I told you before, the prom really isn't my thing."

He's upset, Jordan knew. *That's why he won't look at me.* "I didn't think so. Okay. Well, um, see you around," Jordan said, backing onto the sidewalk and not knowing what else to say. At the same time, she was horrified by the sense of relief she was feeling, relief that Shane didn't want to go to the prom with Tara.

Why? How? What was going on inside her? It was all so confusing.

As Shane peeled away, Jordan turned and headed up the front path to her house, trying not to imagine what it would feel like to kiss Shane's beautiful lips. She realized that she was still wearing Shane's jacket and pulled it around her to keep the chill of the night air at bay. Could it be that deep down, in her inner soul, Jordan wanted to keep Shane all to herself?

CHAPTER *Thirteen*

From Freak to Fabulous

(a three-tiered plan for Victor Kaminski)

Tier 1: Organize and Purge

a) *Check wardrobe restructuring possibilities*

b) *Dispose of dorky temptations (i.e., penny loafers,*
tight pants, Star Trek memorabilia, etc.)

Tier 2: Strategic Shopping

a) *Replace garments as needed (new glasses*
ASAP)

b) *Direct how to mix and match **

*Basics only — advanced fashion not possible within time
span

164

Tier 3: Perfect the Look
a) *Haircut/separation of eyebrows/*
   convince to facial?
b) *Discuss cool factor (walk, talk, etc.)***
c) *Intro. to coordination/can subject*
   dance?

**No more calling himself K-man!!!

Tara dipped her pinkie into a pot of cherry-flavored gloss and swiped it over her lips as she reviewed her plan to transform Victor from a dorky jokester to hot and sexy dream date. She leaned against a row of lockers across from the school auditorium, waiting for him.

So what if he wasn't exactly the fantasy prom king she'd been envisioning since freshman year. Sometimes a girl had to be realistic about things — and the reality was that Victor "K-Man" Kaminski had potential . . . or at least Tara hoped that he did. Whatever. The *important* thing was that

Victor was willing to be molded, and Tara had an idea of who she could model him after — none other than Mr. Prom King himself, Nate Lombardo. *I'm sure Jordan won't mind,* Tara thought.

Actually, the whole thing was sort of a win-win if it all worked out. Not only would Tara gain a decent date for the prom, Victor would be left to wield his brand-new social skills and fashion sense just in time for college.

You can do this, she thought, psyching herself up for the job. *Victor can't be that bad.*

"Hey, babe. The K-Man is here, at your service," Victor said, swaggering down the hall and looking *pretty* pleased with himself.

Tara rolled her eyes, gave him a once-over, and cringed: frizzy pseudo-mullet plus unibrow plus crooked glasses plus clothes that looked as if he had worn them to bed *three nights in a row*? What was she thinking when she said she'd go to prom with *him*? Didn't she notice all that back in the lunchroom yesterday? *Oh, God*, she thought. *There's no way I can pull this off.*

But what were her options?

"Right. Um, let's set a few ground rules to start, okay?" Tara began, and Victor nodded. "Good. Number one: Please don't ever refer to yourself in third person. It's weird. Number two: Don't call yourself K-Man. I don't know who made up that nickname, but it's also weird. Number three — now pay attention because this one is very important — my name is Tara, not *babe*. Got it?"

Victor gave her a mock salute and clicked his heels. "Yes, sir."

Oh . . . God. Tara sighed and pushed open the doors that led to the student parking lot as she considered the task ahead of her. This was way more serious than she'd originally thought. Victor's dorkdom was present not only on the surface; it went deep down to the core.

To make matters worse, when they arrived at the hood of an old orange heap of

167

junk in the parking lot that Tara thought must have been abandoned because nobody in their right mind would be caught dead riding in it, Victor informed her that she would, in fact, be riding in it — *alive*. It was his car.

She opened the door to find CDs, papers, soda cans, and books on the passenger seat and strewn about the entire vehicle. "*Where am I supposed to sit?*" Tara asked.

"Oh. Sorry." Victor pushed the pile onto the backseat. "Don't worry about the stuff on the floor," he said. "Just step on it."

Gingerly climbing inside, Tara was immediately struck by an unpleasant scent that she could only imagine was fermenting sour cream (since she'd never had the pleasure of actually smelling fermenting sour cream). *Ew. He doesn't have an old taco in here somewhere, does he?* she wondered as Victor jogged around the front of the car, then climbed in as well.

"Where to, T-Bone?" he asked, starting the engine.

"T-Bone?" Tara recoiled. "Uh, no. You are *so* not calling me that. What's with the stupid nicknames, anyway?"

Victor scoffed. "Tara, I was only kidding. Come on. Lighten up on the attitude, will you? This is supposed to be fun."

"Attitude?" Tara echoed. "Fun?" Obviously the boy had no clue how much work he needed to be considered even remotely prom-ready . . . but she *supposed* that she could ease up on the snark. "Fine," Tara told him. "Let's go to your house. I need to see what I'm working with, clotheswise. And you need to change. We can't go shopping in that," she added, referring to his wrinkled button-down and jeans that were a tad too short, exposing his sockless ankles and a pair of, surprisingly, cool blue Vans. *At least he's not wearing penny loafers,* she thought.

"No, no, no . . . maybe, no . . ." Tara said, sitting perched atop a dresser in Victor's room as he pulled various items of clothing off the floor of his closet and showed them to her for approval. Despite the fact that his wardrobe was devoid of loafers, the Victor Kaminski fashion salvage wasn't salvaging much. In fact, aside from an interesting collection of vintage sneakers, it seemed as though the Emerson mascot was going to need a Complete Style Overhaul.

Tara glanced around the messy room as Victor moved from the stuff in his closet to the stuff on the floor. He held up a long-sleeved yellow tee that had the quote "Live Long and Prosper" on it.

"How 'bout this one?" he asked.

"Sorry." Tara shook her head. "No *Star Trek* allowed." She tried to decipher what color his rug was. She thought it could be beige but wasn't sure, due to the fact that it was covered with the aftermath of the apparent bomb that must have gone off in his room.

How could one person be so disorganized? she wondered. Actually, it was pretty amazing when she thought about it.

"I know I have a clean shirt around here somewhere," Victor said, plowing through a mound of clothes on his bed.

"You know, I think we should start fresh," Tara said. "Maybe your mom has done laundry lately?" she suggested.

"Good idea. I'll check the laundry room," Victor said, and was out and back in a flash with a basket of clean clothes.

Tara picked out a basic white T-shirt and a pair of passable jeans. They'd worry about organizing and purging his closet later. Victor's wardrobe was about to be reborn.

"What's next, Tara?" Victor asked in the mall three hours later. Shopping bags in hand, he raced in front of her like an anxious little puppy.

Tara had decided that the best approach to Victor's look was to work around the only cool part of his wardrobe — his sneakers. So they wound up going with a layering of vintage-y, preppy looks, mixing lots of casual shirts and tees and loose pants with a couple of tailored sweaters and an awesome 1970s-inspired jacket.

The clothes worked on Victor's lean frame . . . sort of. Something was off, and Tara couldn't quite put her finger on what it was. She suspected that it had to do with the boy's crooked eyewear and unmanageable 'do. Tara wasn't about to let Victor get his hair cut in a mall, but they *could* get some new specs. "Let's go to House of Eyeglasses," Tara replied.

Once in the store, Victor gravitated toward a pair of ugly black-framed glasses almost identical to the ones he was wearing. "Why don't we try a pair of wire frames?" Tara suggested, handing him some of elegant rectangular glasses.

Victor slid them on and slid them off. "Not comfortable."

"Let's go for something a little funkier in plastic then." She picked out chunky brown frame with thick sides, which Victor didn't like. He proceeded to try on frame after frame. After Victor rejected what seemed like the millionth pair, he put on his own glasses and said, "Why don't I just wear my contacts?"

Tara stared at him, stunned. "You have contacts? How come I always see you in these?" she asked, gesturing to the spectacles resting lopsided on his nose.

Victor shrugged. "I'm not a morning person. I can't be bothered putting them in before school."

"Let me see something," Tara said, reaching up to take off Victor's hideous glasses. It was the first time she realized how tall he was — maybe 6'2". It was also the first time that Tara noticed Victor's thoughtful hazel eyes.

Not bad for a guy with a unibrow, she thought. *Not bad at all.*

CHAPTER *Fourteen*

On Wednesday afternoon, Jordan filled Nisha in on her exciting escapade with Shane over cinnamon mocha lattes in the school's courtyard. "I knew my mom was going to be upset when I got home last night, but Nate calling my house twice didn't help any," she said, sitting cross-legged in the grass. "To make things worse, when my mom asked where I'd been, I told her I was with you but she totally knew that I was lying. I think she has ESP."

"Nope, she called my house." Nisha took a sip of her coffee. "I was the one who answered the phone . . . thank *God*.

Otherwise my parents would have had a ton of questions," she said.

Jordan winced. "Sorry about that."

"No, it's totally fine," Nisha replied. "I was home from Brian's by the time she called. I tried to cover for you, but my mom caught me off guard. Why didn't you give me a heads-up, Jordan? Maybe I could have come up with something better than the standard 'She's in the bathroom' line."

Jordan sighed. "I don't know. I guess I didn't think it through. I didn't think *anything* through yesterday," she muttered under her breath.

Nisha regarded her closely. "Jordan, did something *happen* between you and Shane?"

"No. Why? What makes you say that?" Jordan asked, hoping she wasn't trying too hard to seem surprised by Nisha's question.

Nisha placed a hand on Jordan's shoulder. "Come on. It's me you're talking to. There has to be a reason why you wanted to meet after school, just the two of us."

Jordan knew Nisha was right about that. Jordan had to talk to somebody, but she didn't know where to begin. "Nothing happened really, but . . ." Jordan trailed off. "Promise you won't tell Tara? I don't want to hear 'I told you so' from her."

Nisha nodded. "I swear on all that is sacred and pure," she said, holding up three fingers of her right hand in the Girl Scout salute. "Now, spill it."

"It's just that I feel so guilty. Shane and I . . . when he was dropping me off at home . . . we . . . we almost kissed."

"What?!" Nisha shouted, then glanced around to see if the other students milling around had noticed. She turned back to Jordan. "What?" she said again, this time whispering.

"We didn't," Jordan explained. "I *wanted* to," she added. "But I couldn't. I kept thinking about Nate."

As if on cue, Nate strolled into the courtyard looking cute and casual in a striped rugby shirt and a pair of loose-fitting khakis.

Jordan gulped. "Oh, no. Baseball practice must be over early. There he is," she murmured to Nisha. "Let's get out of here before he sees us." Jordan knew that she'd have to face Nate eventually, but she wasn't ready to do so now. She and Nisha quickly gathered their things.

"Uh, I think it's too late for that," Nisha said, pausing.

"Hey, guys!" Nate called, and Jordan turned to see him waving and crossing the grass in their direction.

"I'm gonna head off," Nisha said, heaving her backpack over her shoulder and standing. "Good luck, okay? Call me later." She waved to Nate, spun around, and headed for the school building.

Jordan forced a smile. "Hey! Nate! Hi! What's up?" she said when he'd reached her.

"What's up?" Nate asked, looking upset. "Shouldn't you tell me? What happened to you yesterday? You totally bailed on Antonio's."

That's what he's angry about? That I didn't go to the pizza place with him? No 'I was so worried about you because you disappeared out of thin air'? Jordan thought, which kind of irritated her. Here she was feeling guilty for almost hurting her boyfriend, while all along all he was thinking about was pizza?

"You know, I could have been kidnapped or in an accident or worse and all you're worried about is that I didn't make it to your precious Antonio's?" Jordan burst out. "Thanks for your concern."

Nate shifted his backpack. "Are you serious?" he asked. "I knew you weren't in an accident —"

"Yeah, because you called my house about a million times," Jordan said, interrupting him. "Thanks for that, too. I'm grounded for the rest of the week because of you. Why did you have to call my mother?"

"Because you weren't answering your cell phone, that's why!" Nate cried.

"So you were so worried that I couldn't accompany you to a pizza place that you had

178

to bother my mother?" Jordan shot back. "It was that important?"

"Look Jordan, I don't know what your problem is, but —" Nate said.

"My *problem* is you spying on me," Jordan replied, not letting him finish. "And I don't like it."

"Oh, yeah? Well, I don't like *you*, right now," Nate said, backing up. "Call me when the evil pill you took today wears off, okay?"

Jordan swallowed hard, stung by the comment. *Nate's right. I am being mean . . . and unfair.* She stared after him as he stormed across the grass and toward the student parking lot. *What am I doing? Why am I fighting with my boyfriend for no reason?* she asked herself.

Jordan already knew the answer.

Shane.

That evening Jordan sat cross-legged on the rug staring blankly at the pictures strewn around her. She was trying to compile a series for her introspective, but she was having trouble concentrating on photography. Actually, she'd been having a major problem focusing — period. Her mind kept wandering to that stupid argument with Nate in the courtyard. Whenever she would try to compose a decent apology, her thoughts would drift back to her evening with Shane — their easy conversation in Eggersville Park, dancing wildly to punk rock music in Chicago and not caring who was watching . . . but then Jordan would linger on their almost-kiss at the end of their adventure. She fantasized about what Shane's lips would have felt like — sometimes scolding herself, other times, wishing that she'd had the guts to find out. She tried hiding the pictures of their trip in her desk drawer, but even that couldn't stop her mind from wandering back to the unknown. She had never experienced a pull to kiss someone as strong as it had been with Shane. It wasn't only a physical thing. Jordan sensed it was deeper than that. But how was it possible to feel this way with a boy she'd known for less than a week?

Then there was Nate. Jordan wasn't stupid; she knew that girls at school totally envied what she had with him. And she knew that Nate truly cared for her — that was for sure. Of course Jordan loved him, too, and she was definitely attracted to him — who wouldn't be? She and Nate had so much in common, like sports and similar friends — not to mention the fact that they'd probably be voted prom king and queen. Was she really willing to throw away a solid year-and-a-half relationship for some crazy magnetic lust for a guy she barely knew?

Jordan sighed. She couldn't think about it anymore. She stared at the mess on her rug and picked up a photograph. "I have to work on my project," she said aloud, even though she wasn't in the mood.

Jordan was grateful when a knock sounded at her door. "Come on in, Mom," she called.

The door creaked open, but Nate's face peeked into her room. "Hey," Jordan said quietly, glad that he was here to talk, but afraid of what he might say.

"Your mom let me in." Nate stepped into the room, but stayed by the door. "I wanted to talk to you about . . . you know."

Jordan nodded and motioned for him to come in.

Nate closed the door, left his backpack by the foot of her desk, and crossed around the photos to sit beside her.

"I'm sorry," Jordan blurted out as soon as he was settled.

"I'm sorry," Nate said at the same time, and they both chuckled.

"I wasn't spying on you, Jordan, and I wasn't angry that you didn't show up for pizza. I was worried," Nate said. "It's not like you to just go off somewhere and not tell anybody."

Jordan nodded. "I know . . . and I know you weren't spying on me," she admitted. "I guess I just said that because I was upset about being grounded. I was taking it out on you when it wasn't your fault at all." *It was mine*, she thought. *All mine.*

"Don't worry about it," Nate said, reaching an arm around her. "We all have our bad days, right?"

Jordan nodded. How could she have considered being with someone else when she had such an understanding boyfriend? Her throat tightened. "I'm really sorry, Nate," she said, feeling the sting of tears behind her eyes. "I'm sorry for everything. It'll never happen again. I promise."

"Hey, hey. What's this?" he asked, touching her cheek with his hand — the same place that Shane had touched the night before. Nate clearly had no idea how much Jordan was apologizing for. "Don't cry. Really. It's okay." He gave her a reassuring hug. "Nobody's perfect."

He's got that right, Jordan thought.

"I just hope your adventure was worth being grounded," Nate added. "So are you going to tell me about it, or what?" He pulled a goofy face, which made her laugh.

Jordan told Nate all about her road trip to see *Vert et Vrai* in Eggersville and then the Violent Kittens in Chicago, though she substituted for Shane some fictitious girl named Sharon who apparently went to Southside High. Then she and Nate turned to Jordan's photography project. They laughed, going through the old photos, reminiscing about the good times they'd had when they were taken. Nate seemed genuinely interested in the new pictures, too, and made suggestions about how she might use them in her project.

Soon they were lying on her bed and listening to music. Nate was so easy to be with, so free with his affection. And when Nate leaned in to kiss her it felt safe and familiar and warm.

He was a good guy — a *really* good guy. How could she possibly think of messing things up with him, especially with the prom so close?

CHAPTER *Fifteen*

Hair Removal Techniques

1) *Beg Sergio to squeeze in Victor's appt.*
2) *Go through mags. 4 ideas and/or snag pic. of Nate 4 reference*
3) *Don't mention eyebrow wax till last min.*
4) *Good-bye unibrow (don't call us, we'll call u)*

"You're a lifesaver, Sergio. Thanks for taking us," Tara breathed into her handheld after school on Wednesday. "This is a major hair emergency. You'll see what I mean when we get there."

"Anything for you, my darling," Sergio cooed. "You bring your little friend to me and I will turn him into a new man."

Could you turn him into Nate Lombardo? Tara wanted to ask. *Ah, if only it were possible.* It wasn't. Aside from Victor's nice eyes, Tara knew that there was little else for the stylist Sergio Vonhugel to work with. "Thanks again, Sergio. See you in a few!"

Tara hung up her phone and found a semi-clean spot on Victor's orange car to lean on while she waited for him to show up. She checked her watch. They had to leave soon if they were to make it to the Sergio Salon on time.

Tara's phone rang. She cringed when she saw Jenny Brigger's name pop up onto the screen. "Hello?" she answered crisply.

"Yeah, hi," Jenny said. "I'll need you to pick up a pizza for the prom meeting this afternoon."

First of all, Tara wasn't a gofer. Second of all . . . "What prom meeting?" she demanded, annoyed. "I didn't set up a meeting."

"Oh, I did that on my own. Sorry. I must have forgotten to mention it," Jenny said with what sounded to Tara like a hint of satisfaction in her voice. "Anyway, we're meeting with the theater tech guys to see if they can build a gigantic castle to look like the one they have down in Disney World."

Tara was glad that Jenny couldn't see the gagging gesture she was making right then. "Um, Jenny . . . isn't that taking 'Once Upon a Time' too literally?" she asked. What was next? Getting someone to dress like Cinderella and hand out table numbers? "Look, the theme can work, but only if you go figuratively. We can make the room look romantic with linen choices and colorful tulle . . . not castles and storybook constructions. That's a waste of money."

Tara heard Jenny's loud sigh over the line. "We all agreed yesterday that this is the way we're going."

"Yesterday?" Tara repeated through gritted teeth.

"Oh." Jenny giggled. "I guess I forgot to mention that meeting, too. Sorry. Anyway, you should be at my house by four — and don't forget the pepperoni. Bye!"

Tara would like to tell Jenny what she could do with her pepperoni, but she was too much of a lady to do so. And she hated to see the prom morphing into this . . . cheese-fest. But what could Tara do? She was out-numbered. Tara didn't want to quit, but she didn't want her good name to be associated with a prom disaster either.

"What's the matter?" Victor asked.

Tara had been so caught up in her thoughts that she hadn't noticed that he was standing there. She was glad to see that Victor was wearing his contacts, but his new clothes were a mess. "What happened to you?" she cried, gesturing to his wrinkled white cotton pants and his green-and-white short-sleeved polo shirt with the purple jelly stain on it.

"Nothing." Victor shrugged as he checked out his outfit, then noticed the stain. "Oops. That was lunch."

Tara shook her head and entered Victor's car. Clearly she had more work ahead of her . . . but at least the inside of his car was cleaned out. That was a sign of progress, right?

On the way to Sergio's, Tara explained the situation with Jenny Brigger and the awful turn the prom was taking. "Maybe I should just quit," Tara said, feeling near tears. "That's what Jenny wants me to do, and nobody is listening to me, anyway."

"You can't quit. The prom will be a nightmare if we let Jenny have her way," Victor said, turning right at an intersection. "I know her. She's a total control freak. Somehow we have to get her to think that the *good* ideas are coming from her head."

Tara turned to him. "We?" she asked. "Are you offering your help?"

Victor's cheeks turned bright pink. "Well, only if you want it," he said.

"You'd do that for me?" she asked, pleased by the gesture, but also confused by it. "Why?" Most guys didn't care enough about the prom to offer what was sure to be hours and hours of their time.

"Come on, Tara. Why wouldn't I?" Victor said. "I mean, you're helping me, aren't you?"

In a way, Tara guessed that she was, though truthfully she knew this makeover was more for her than for Victor. *I guess Victor doesn't see it that way.* "Thanks," she told him. "That's really cool of you."

"No problem," Victor said, then swung a right into the Sergio Salon lot and parked.

Tara noticed that Victor grew suddenly quiet the moment they entered the sleek salon. "Are you nervous?" she asked as they took a seat on a white leather couch positioned along a shiny brown laminate wall. "Don't be. Sergio's the best."

"Ah, there you are," Sergio called, welcoming them as he adjusted the knit black hat on his bald head. It complemented the tight black tee he was wearing underneath an unbuttoned pale blue western shirt, as well as the designer jeans he had on.

Tara rose to greet him with a kiss on each cheek. "This is the guy I was telling you about." She gestured to Victor, who was now standing next to her.

Sergio squinted at the boy, and Tara could practically see the wheels turning. "I think we should just shave it all off and start new," Sergio said finally.

"No!" Victor burst out, both hands clutching his frizzy hair.

"Um, maybe we don't want to take it all off," Tara said, worried about Victor's minor freak-out. "How about if we . . . do this?" She rooted through her purse for a picture of Nate she'd found in her album the night before, and showed it to the stylist.

Sergio examined the picture and nodded. "Yes, we can do this. Certainly," he said, handing back the photo. "Come with me, my friend," he said to Victor.

As Sergio guided a nervous Victor toward

the back of the salon, Tara remembered something else. "Oh, Sergio, one more thing," she said. "Could you have one of the girls . . . you know?" She touched the skin in between her eyebrows. "Clean him up a little bit?"

Sergio nodded. "Say no more, Tara. We'll take care of everything," he said, then disappeared with Victor into the heart of the salon.

Great! Tara thought, crossing the Victor's eyebrow waxing off her list. Then she went to the Starbucks next door for a latte while Victor's makeover took place. With coffee in hand, she sat in a comfy purple club chair by the window and reviewed the three-tiered plan she had created. The next tier involved finding out if Victor could dance. *I'll have to do that one delicately,* Tara said to herself. *And I should probably wait a couple of days.* She had a feeling that Victor might be somewhat traumatized by the haircut and eyebrow waxing and would probably need a break from his makeover. *Maybe I should get him coffee or something as a peace offering,* she thought. *He really is being a good sport about all this.*

About forty-five minutes later Tara left Starbucks with a latte for Victor and two giant chocolate-chip cookies in a bag. She was dying to see how the haircut had turned out.

She entered the salon and found Victor, sitting in a Sergio's orange styling chair with his back toward her, chatting casually with the hairdresser.

Victor's hair looked clean and cropped closely in the back. *It doesn't seem too bad from this angle,* Tara thought.

Sergio glanced up from the conversation, noticing Tara's presence. "Ah, you're back," he said. "I think you're going to like the new look."

Anything's got to be better than before, Tara thought. She waited anxiously as Sergio spun the chair around so that Victor could face her.

Tara dropped the bag she was holding

when she saw him. Victor now had a cool, closely cropped cut — with just enough on top to tousle into a cute faux-hawk if he wanted. The new cut exposed an angular jaw that one would expect to see only on a male model. His eyebrows — his *two* eyebrows — were clean, yet still masculine, turning what Tara had once thought were thoughtful eyes into two piercing hazel pools of mystery that were suddenly giving her shivers.

"Do you like it?" Victor asked, awkwardly rising out of the seat.

Tara couldn't respond. All she kept thinking was . . .

Victor Kaminski . . . he . . . he's gorgeous!

CHAPTER *Sixteen*

"So? How do I look?" Brian asked Nisha as he emerged from the dressing room at Tuxedo Depot wearing a shiny white tux with tails. He held out his arms and did a little dance turn for her.

"Like an ice-cream man who takes his job way too seriously?" Nisha offered, giggling and hoping that her boyfriend wasn't serious about the suit. "What else do you have in there?"

Brian opened the mirrored door to his dressing room, went inside, and returned a few minutes later sporting a traditional single-breasted black jacket with matching flat-front pants. Underneath the jacket he wore a white shirt and a cream-colored vest that made the suit stand out from the others.

This time Nisha's jaw dropped. Brian didn't resemble a psycho ice-cream guy *or* a penguin. He looked totally hot! Seeing him all dressed up made Nisha want to wrap her arms around him right there and slow dance in the middle of Tuxedo Depot. "Wow, you look amazing," she murmured.

"Should we rent this one?" Brian asked as he fixed his lapels. Nisha nodded enthusiastically.

She called over a nearby salesman to take Brian's measurements. When the salesman was finished, Brian disappeared back in the dressing room to change into his jeans and T-shirt. Ten minutes later, Brian had filled out a form, put down a deposit on the tuxedo, and they were leaving the store and heading into the mall.

Nisha slid her cell phone out of her pocket to check the time. "That has to have been some kind of record," she told Brian. "You took a total of twenty-six minutes to choose and rent your tux for the prom. I've been shopping for a dress for weeks — and still am. Guys definitely have it easier. All you have to do is point to a picture in a catalog, try on a jacket or two, get your measurements taken, and pick up your tux the day before the prom."

"Well, at least one of us will look good on prom night," Brian said, giving her a nudge.

Nisha swatted his arm playfully as they passed Nordstrom. Nisha wondered if she should show Brian the yellow chiffon dress she had on hold but decided against it. Wasn't it bad luck for the date to see the dress before the prom or something?

"Hey, let's go in Godiva for a minute," Brian suggested, swerving into the store next to Nordstrom.

Nisha followed him inside, happily breathing in the sweet aroma of chocolate. She stared at a wall of shelves filled from top to bottom with delectable treats housed in golden boxes. "Mmm. I love fancy chocolates," she said, making her way to the glass cases where the individual candies were displayed, her mouth watering. "I'm only allowing myself one today . . . three at the most. I like the kind with the hazelnut cream in the middle."

"Do your think your parents would like this?" Brian picked a medium-sized box from a shelf and held it thoughtfully. "I figured I'd bring some by when I meet them this weekend . . . or is that too obviously sucking up?" he asked.

Nisha knew that she should be thrilled about her boyfriend trying so hard to impress her parents. Instead, she panicked. She thought that if she never mentioned meeting her parents again, Brian would just forget about it. Clearly she'd been wrong about that. "Um, I don't think they like chocolate," she fibbed.

"Are you kidding?" Brian asked. "Who doesn't like chocolate?"

Nisha shrugged, not knowing what else to say. All she knew was that Brian could not meet her parents this weekend — or any weekend. What was she going to do? The overpowering scent of chocolate suddenly turned from delectable to nauseating, making her feel sick to her stomach.

"Hey, are you all right?" Brian asked Nisha, placing a hand on her arm. "You look a little pale."

"I don't feel so well," she told him. "Maybe I should go home."

"Sure." Brian hurriedly put back the Godiva box and led Nisha to his car.

Nisha's head spun for the entire drive as she tried to think of a good excuse for Brian not to come over this weekend, but her mind was blank. At least she knew that her mother wouldn't be home this afternoon, so Brian could drop her off in front of the house instead of a few blocks away.

"So if your parents don't like chocolate," Brian was saying as he approached her street, "maybe I should just bring flowers like you did to my house." He paused, and then his whole face lit up. "Oh, I know! I can ask my mom if she'll bake one of her famous Irish soda breads. What do you think, Nisha?"

"I don't think you should go to all that trouble, Brian," Nisha told him. What she *really* wanted to say was, *I don't think you should go to all that trouble because you won't be meeting my parents*, but she couldn't bring herself to do it. "Besides, my parents are so boring," she tagged on instead. "Why don't we do something fun instead? Just the two of us?"

Brian parked the car and faced her, his brow furrowed. "Nisha? Is there something you want to tell me?" he asked.

Yes! "No," she replied, her hand searching for the door handle so she could get out of there.

"Are you ashamed of me?" Brian blurted out as she opened the door. "Because it really seems like you are. You make excuses for me to drop you off blocks from your house, and now you're acting as if you don't want me to meet your parents."

"No, it's not that," Nisha said, knowing that she couldn't put it off any longer. She had to come clean. "I'd never be ashamed of you. It's just . . ." She paused, trying to find the right words then deciding to take the simple, straightforward route. "You're not Indian," she told him.

Brian released a breath, seeming relieved. "Is that all?" he asked. "I'm sure they'll like me once they get to know me."

Nisha shook her head. Brian wasn't getting it. "That's just it," she said. "You could be the greatest guy in the world, but it doesn't change the fact that you're not Indian." Nisha knew that was only part of the problem, but she truly believed that if Brian were named Sanit or Deepak her parents would have an easier time getting over the whole secret-boyfriend thing.

"Ah, but how many Indian guys have my wit and charm?" Brian asked, complete with pointing an index finger in the air. "I promise you, they won't be able to resist me." He grinned. "You couldn't, right?"

Nisha smiled and leaned in to kiss him. "You're right about that," she conceded, although she could guarantee that her parents would be a much tougher sell than she was.

After Nisha said good-bye to Brian, she entered her house even more worried about the coming weekend than before. Brian didn't grasp the severity of the situation. How could he? *Maybe I should just let him come over this weekend and see what happens,* she mused, heading straight for her bedroom and flopping onto her canopied bed. *It would be nice to have it all out in the open for once.*

But Nisha knew how her parents felt about dating. Introducing them to Brian would probably feel like a slap in the face to them. They'd be devastated — not to mention furious — when they found out she'd been going behind their backs all this time, and Nisha would be crushed. How could she hurt them like that? And if she decided not to go through with it, she'd have to make up another excuse to Brian. Would he even believe her this time?

Nisha glanced at the phone on her nightstand, wishing she could talk to Jordan and Tara about it, but she knew that, just like Brian, they wouldn't completely understand her dilemma. There was only one person who could possibly comprehend what she was faced with — Kali. Nisha's sister had dated plenty of American boys; surely she'd know what to do.

Deciding that the problem was way too complicated for an e-mail, Nisha quickly calculated the time difference to London. It was late over there, but she remembered that her sister was a night owl and dialed the number anyway.

"What's wrong?" Kali asked almost immediately after picking up the phone, knowing that Nisha was more likely to send a transatlantic text or IM than to call.

Forgetting all the niceties, Nisha got straight to the point. "I need your perspective," she said, then launched into the whole complicated story. How she'd been dating Brian for six months and how they were preparing for prom. How her guru caught her kissing Brian at the Todi Studio and threatened to tell Mom and Dad. About how welcoming Brian's family had been when they'd met her. And finally about how Brian wanted to meet the parents this weekend. "So now, I'm not only lying to Mom and Dad, I'll be lying to Brian. I don't know how much longer I can keep it up," Nisha finished, and waited anxiously for Kali's response.

Kali was quiet for a moment. "Nisha, this isn't such a serious problem," she said finally. "I know exactly how you should handle it."

"Really?" Nisha asked, surprised. *Kali's probably going to tell me to be honest with everybody*, she thought. *That's always the easiest solution.*

"Whatever you do," Kali said, "*Don't* introduce the American boy to Mom and Dad."

Nisha wanted to burst into tears.

"Kali!" Nisha cried. "But then I have to keep lying to Brian. I don't think I can do it for much longer."

"Please. Take your sister's advice," Kali said. "Go to the prom with your boyfriend. Have a wonderful time. But I'm telling you, it's not worth the heartache of introducing him to the family," she added. "Remember what happened to me during my junior year, when I told Mom about Todd?"

How could Nisha could forget it? She was around ten years old and fascinated by Todd's long locks and fast motorcycle. However, her sister did mix up one part of the story. "You didn't *tell* Mom," Nisha reminded her. "She caught you hiding Todd in the laundry room." It was the first time Nisha had ever seen her parents go ballistic. Needless to say, Kali's relationship with Todd ended immediately, and so did her social life for about six months. "Plus Brian is nothing like Todd." Nisha put in, knowing that it probably didn't make a difference.

"Listen to me, Nisha," Kali said soothingly. "You and Brian will be going to the prom in a few weeks. The last days of high school will fly by after that. Before you know it, you and Brian be attending separate colleges, and eventually, the romance will end. Case closed."

Nisha listened carefully to everything her sister had to say, knowing that Kali was speaking from experience.

However, there was one chink in her wisdom.

What if Nisha didn't *want* it to end with Brian?

"'Wherever go the hands, so follows the gaze of the eyes. Wherever go the eyes, so follows the attunement of the mind. Wherever goes the mind, so follows the expression of feeling. Wherever goes the feeling, so follows the essence of mood. . . .'"

Nisha whispered her favorite *sloka* the next afternoon as she stood alone, toes pointed outward, in front of the mirrors of the Todi Studio for Indian Classical Dance. Guru Gargi had taught her that saying long ago, when Nisha was first introduced to *Kathak*. It reminded her that a rich performer must always stay connected — body and mind — with the story she was telling.

Although the verse was appropriate for dance, Nisha found it had meaning in life as well. Maybe if she could just focus her mind, her heart would follow. She wouldn't have to worry about Brian and her parents and the prom and her existence after high school. She'd know how to be true to her culture and true to herself at the same time.

The sound of the sitar filled the studio as Nisha slowly crossed her wrists above her head, palms outward, ready to begin her dance. She gracefully slid her arms down her sides, moving them forward until her hands were cupped in front of her. Palms up, she jutted them outward and looked to the heavens as if making an offering to the gods.

Nisha was no longer herself — she was a

girl preparing for a secret rendezvous with her beloved. With fluid motions, she pretended to adorn herself with jewels — a necklace, earrings, bangles on the arms, a quick *tilaka* stain in between her eyebrows. A graceful spin later and she was ready to leave her home, only to cross a hazardous path filled with snakes and demons and other horrifying creatures. With an expression of fear, Nisha leapt and twirled as she avoided each danger. Then a footwork sequence, her bells jangling rhythmically, her arms and hands gesturing as she depicted the girl's treacherous plight. Finally, the dance ended when the girl happily arrived into the arms of her beloved.

Nisha stared at herself in the mirror, breathing hard from the exertion, wondering what would happen next if the story were to continue. Would the girl have to risk her life again in order to get back home? Why was *she* the one who must accept peril in exchange for love? Why not he? And what would happen if they were found out?

Surely the girl would be shamed and shunned by her family — or worse. Was their love worth that?

Nisha stepped closer to the mirror and studied her outfit — a flowing green skirt topped by a matching short blouse called a *choli*, with a green silk *dupatta* wrapped elegantly around the top half of her body. She always wore traditional clothing in the studio. It suited her there, yet it was so different from the American clothes hanging in the dressing room across the hall — the clothes she wore every day. *It's always been easy to change in and out of them*, Nisha thought. *But which one is the costume?* She used to think it was the Indian clothing, but now, after talking to her sister, she wasn't so sure.

Nisha crossed the hall, dressed in her street clothes, and went home. *Maybe I should just take Kali's advice, rather than stir up a big pot of aggravation. She's right. I shouldn't tell my parents about Brian before the prom — or ever,* she thought as she placed her hand on the knob to open the front door to her house. *Now I have to figure out how to break it to Brian*, she said silently. *If only I didn't love him so much . . .*

Mrs. Khubani pulled open the door, surprising Nisha and releasing a delicious wafting aroma of spicy, fried, samosas into the air. "Welcome home, my *Beta*. Did you have a nice practice at the studio?"

"Uh-huh." Nisha noticed that her mother seemed to be in a particularly good mood at the moment. "What's up, Mommy?" she asked, stepping inside.

"Now then, *Beta*, you know that your father and I don't approve of your dating . . ."

Oh, God — no, Nisha thought as she removed her shoes. She had a feeling that despite her mother's smile, this conversation wasn't going to end in a good place. "Yes, I know," she answered cautiously.

"Well, I just met your new friend and I think he's delightful! He's so handsome and well-mannered." Nisha's mother gave her daughter an excited squeeze.

Nisha's brain was whirring. *What? Brian? He's here?*

She didn't know if she should be angry with him for showing up unexpectedly or thrilled that he'd impressed her mother, which was half the battle to winning over her father.

Nisha decided to go with psyched — maybe all her problems were solved!

"Come," her mother said, guiding her toward the living room. "We don't want to keep our special guests waiting!"

Guests? Nisha was confused. Who else was there?

Nisha's questions were answered as soon as she entered the living room. Sitting on the peach-colored couch, munching samosas and sipping tea, was *not* her boyfriend, Brian, as expected, but a tall, handsome Indian boy around her age, and an older couple who looked to be his parents.

Who are these people? What are they doing here? Nisha looked from her mother to the guests and back to her mother again, hoping

211

and praying that this wasn't some sort of arranged meeting. She gulped as the boy rose to greet her.

"Hi, I'm Raj," he said with a friendly smile. "Your mom says you need a date for the prom."

CHAPTER *Seventeen*

"I can't believe you're making me watch this again," Nate said, laughing as the title for the movie *Carrie* appeared on the TV screen in Jordan's living room.

"Oh, I'm sorry," Jordan replied innocently. "Did you want to see *Pretty in Pink* instead?" She pretended to reach for the DVD player. Jordan was obsessed with prom movies — something she knew her boyfriend thought was adorable.

Nate rolled his eyes and laughed again. "C'mere," he said, wrapping an arm around Jordan's shoulders and pulling her back.

Jordan giggled and nuzzled close to him as she relaxed her head onto his shoulder. *It's so easy hanging out with Nate,* she thought, glad that her mother had finally caved on her punishment for going to Chicago.

Chicago. Jordan squeezed her eyes shut, trying to erase the memory of that entire day — of French movies and road trips and punk bands and . . . almost kisses. Jordan had toyed with the idea of telling Nate everything, but then she thought, *Why?* It would only hurt him, and she hadn't actually kissed anybody. She'd been avoiding Shane's calls all week, as well as the text messages about the jacket she'd borrowed, and he'd finally gotten the hint. Now all Jordan had to do was stop *thinking* about him. Once she did that, the guilty feelings would go away and Jordan could concentrate on important things . . . like Nate, the prom, and graduation. . . .

Nate gave Jordan a tender kiss on the top of her head as her cell phone rang. "Aren't you going to get that?" he asked.

Jordan picked up her phone from the end table and cringed when she saw Shane's digits pop up on the screen. "I think it's a wrong number," she said and silenced the phone. *Apparently Shane didn't get the hint yet,* she thought.

Nate reached for some popcorn in the yellow bowl on his lap. "We're all out," he said, frowning.

"I'll make some more. Be right back," Jordan said, grabbing the bowl. "No need to pause the movie, I know what happens." She grinned and headed into the kitchen.

Jordan opened a cabinet and grabbed a bag of popcorn from a shelf. As she threw it into the microwave, a flicker of movement caught her eye outside. Jordan peered through the window over the sink and noticed a blue Mustang idling by the curb in front of her house. *Shane? Oh, God,* she thought as a knot grew in her stomach. *He can't be here. Especially not with Nate in the living room. What is he doing?* Suddenly, she noticed Shane's jacket hanging on the back of a kitchen chair — where she'd left it the other night. *Maybe I should have dealt with this,* she realized. *I'll just give it back to him and then get rid of him as fast as possible.*

Jordan grabbed the finished popcorn from the microwave then pulled Shane's jacket from the chair and went into the living room. She placed the popcorn on the coffee table in front of Nate. "You know what? That was my neighbor on the phone," she told him, trying to keep calm. "I borrowed a jacket from her and now she wants it back. I'll only be a few minutes, okay?"

Nate nodded and seemed satisfied with eating the popcorn for now, so Jordan went back into the kitchen and headed out the side door to confront Shane.

Jordan approached the car carefully as she tried to figure out what to say to him. She decided short and sweet was the best way to go. "Here's your jacket, Shane," she said, handing it to him through the open passenger-side window. "You have to go now."

Shane surprised her by opening his door and stepping out. His eyes earnest, "Jordan," Shane said, "I kind of need to talk to you." He seemed . . . almost hurt.

Jordan felt a pang in her heart, then glanced back at the house. "I can't, Shane. Nate's here. You have to leave."

"Just talk to me for a minute, Jordan," Shane told her. "Hear me out, and then I'll go, I promise."

Jordan didn't want to hear him out. She wanted to run back into the house — back to Nate — but Shane seemed genuinely upset. *I probably should have handled this over the phone the first time he called.* "Fine," she said, trying to keep this businesslike. "What's so important that you had to sit in front of my house like a stalker?"

Shane gazed at her, his dark eyes serious. "I had to tell you that . . . I can't be friends with you."

Jordan scoffed. She was risking her boyfriend catching her in a lie for *that*?

"Are you kidding me? That's it? That's what you have to say?" she asked. "You know, I *would* have gotten the hint if you'd just stopped calling, and it would have been much less dramatic."

Shane shook his head. "No, you don't get it. I can't be *just* friends with you," he said. "I like you too much. I can't stop thinking about Chicago and you and . . . Jordan . . ." His voice trailed off and he took her hand in his.

Jordan glanced away, trying to control the pounding of her heart — the excitement she was feeling over this boy who was only inches away from her. Shane liked her and . . . she liked it.

It's not right. I have to leave. I shouldn't have come out here at all, her head kept saying.

But when Shane leaned in to kiss her, Jordan didn't pull away; she couldn't. And even with Nate inside her house, even though she knew what she was about to do was totally wrong . . . she couldn't help but kiss him back.

Take a sneak peek at what

happens next in the

ONCE UPON A PROM

trilogy!

"It was only a kiss. One stupid kiss. No big deal," Jordan said firmly from her perch on an overstuffed chair at Joes. She uttered the words with such conviction that she surprised herself. To the naked ear, it might have sounded as if Jordan actually *believed* what she was talking about. As if she *hadn't* been up most of last night, cheeks tear-stained from worry and guilt and feeling totally jerk-like for kissing Shane Dresden — a boy who was a friend, yes, but who was, most certainly, *not* her boyfriend. The lovable Nate Lombardo had held that title for the past year-and-a-half. So far.

Nisha was sitting cross-legged on a yellow vintage loveseat wearing her favorite vintage jeans with the perfect hole in the right knee, a crisp white tee, and a pair of cute metallic ballet flats. Jordan squirmed as she watched her friend's almond-shaped eyes go from wide to narrow. "Yeah. Uh-huh. I don't believe you," Nisha said. Apparently the girl did not have a naked ear; she had those supersonic best friend ears that could detect the slightest tone of doubt even if it *was* only in your head.

Not knowing how to reply, Jordan took a long sip of her spicy chai, letting her eyes wander to the old claw-footed bathtub near the bay window, filled with yellowing paperbacks for the taking. She noticed two scruffy-looking boys lounging a couple of seats over — one in black-framed glasses and baggy paint-splattered jeans, the other with a guitar case slung over a wing-backed chair.

The guy with the guitar had a cute shaggy haircut, the color of sand, which was how Jordan always imagined Nate's might look if he let it grow out a little.

Nate. Another pang of guilt pinched her chest.

"Kissing Shane was nothing, all right?" Jordan said. Why couldn't Nisha just believe it? If she did, then maybe, little by little, Jordan could believe it too. "Don't people kiss all the time?" she added with a wave of her chai for emphasis. "Like that foreign exchange student, Paolo. He kisses people twice to say 'hi' then does it again to say 'bye' or whatever. That's, like, four kisses in passing alone. So why does kissing Shane *once* have to be such a big deal?"

Nisha tilted her head, seeming to consider it. "Okay, first of all, Paolo doesn't count. He's *Italian*. His kissing is either totally cultural . . . or he's doing it because he's hot *and* he's got a cute accent so he knows he can get away with it. And second?

I thought you said kissing Shane *wasn't* a big deal."

"Oh, it's not," Jordan assured her. "*So* not. Really, really, not."

"Hmm." Nisha placed her enormous cup of peach tea lemonade on a metal end table and leaned forward. "I guess that's why you can't stop talking about it, huh?"

"Fine," Jordan replied. "From this moment forward I'll refrain from ever mentioning Shane Dresden and/or his lips again. See?" She pretended to close an invisible zipper over her mouth. But the truth was, Jordan wanted to go on forever about how kissing Shane wasn't a big deal because she knew that when she was finally quiet she'd have to deal with reality: That last night she may have accidentally flushed her relationship with Nate down the toilet.

Voted Most Likely to Live Happily Ever After in the school yearbook, Nate was on the football *and* baseball teams, while Jordan led the cheerleading squad to national victory. They were so popular it was a given that they'd be crowned prom king and queen in a couple of weeks. And Jordan adored Nate's boyish charm, not to mention the fact that he was completely gorgeous and caring and, oh yeah, *loyal.*

Nate's every girl's fantasy. So what's my problem? Why didn't I walk away from Shane last night? Why did I have to . . . kiss him?

"Oh, Nisha, I feel *awful.*" What was the point of still pretending? She wasn't fooling anyone. "I mean, there Nate was, being all super-boyfriendy in my den, munching on microwave popcorn and watching a movie that I'd picked out. And where was I? I was making out with Shane right at the end of my driveway." She covered her face with her hands, feeling the familiar sting of tears behind her eyes. "God, could I be more evil?"

"You're *not* evil, Jord. You didn't go out there intending to make out with the guy," Nisha reminded her. "He said he wanted his jacket back and you went to return it *and* to tell him to get the hint — that you're with Nate."

It was true. And Jordan *wanted* to be with Nate, but there was something about Shane that stirred her every time she saw him. The boy may have been unconventional-looking with his uneven jet-black hair and nail polish to match, but he was also poetic and intense. Jordan found herself strangely attracted to him — and tempted — which was why she'd stopped returning his calls.

"I didn't mean for it to happen," she said, looking up. "We started off as friends. Then something, I don't know, it *shifted*." She willed herself not to lose it in the middle of the teahouse but tears trickled down her cheeks anyway. "I just never thought I'd be a cheater, you know?"

Nisha leaned forward, putting a hand on Jordan's knee. "Things happen, Jord. People make mistakes." She handed her a brown paper napkin. "Here."

Jordan dried her eyes, grateful to have such a good friend. Ever since second grade, right or wrong, Nisha had always had her back. But Jordan knew she had to make this good again somehow. Should she pour her heart out to Nate and beg his forgiveness? Hold it all inside and hope that he never found out? Break up?

"Look, maybe it's like you said," Nisha went on, "one kiss shouldn't be a big deal."

"It *shouldn't* . . ." Jordan trailed off as she remembered Shane's soft, cherry-colored lips—a warm contrast against his pale skin and mysterious dark eyes. How he'd gently stroked her hair before leaning in to kiss her. How she'd welcomed the feel of his arms as they lingered in an embrace. Jordan's heart had felt as if it might have thumped right out of her chest from beating so hard.

"Oh, boy," Nisha said. "By the look on your face, I gather Shane's lip-lock was pretty good?"

"Unforgettable," Jordan admitted. "That's the problem." *But is it worth giving up Nate for?*

"So what are you going to do?" Nisha asked.

"I have to choose," Jordan replied, though it sounded strange saying it out loud. Choose who? There was only one choice: the boy who'd been there since junior year. The cute, easy-going guy who could make her laugh in an instant. The one who *knew* her and liked her friends. She couldn't imagine slow dancing at the prom with anyone else.

"Nate?" Nisha asked hopefully, and Jordan nodded.

"Right now I can't see myself without him, and I don't think I want to."

"Not to mention that the whole school would probably riot if you guys broke up right before prom," Nisha half-joked.

"Yeah, there's that too," Jordan said. To the students at Emerson High, she and Nate were like Oreos and milk, sun and sand, Dolce and Gabanna; they were just good together, no questions asked. So what if she and Shane had chemistry? Jordan and Nate had that and more. They had history. And fun. And trust . . . well, until recently. "Maybe we should keep what happened with Shane between us. Telling Nate will only hurt him, and for what?" She paused, reflecting. "I was probably just infatuated with Shane because he's so different from the other the guys I know, anyway. Now that I've kissed him, it's like he's out of my system, right? So I'm over it."

Nisha raised her eyebrows. "You sure about that?"

I know I want to be, Jordan thought. "I'm sure," she said. "And what harm could one little secret do?"

To Do List: Read all the Point books!

By Aimee Friedman

- ❏ South Beach
- ❏ French Kiss
- ❏ Hollywood Hills
- ❏ The Year My Sister Got Lucky

- ❏ Oh Baby!
  By Randi Reisfeld and H.B. Gilmour

. . . .

- ❏ Hotlanta
  By Denene Millner and Mitzi Miller

By Hailey Abbott

- ❏ Summer Boys
- ❏ Next Summer: A Summer Boys Novel
- ❏ After Summer: A Summer Boys Novel
- ❏ Last Summer: A Summer Boys Novel

By Claudia Gabel

- ❏ In or Out
- ❏ Loves Me, Loves Me Not: An In or Out Novel
- ❏ Sweet and Vicious: An In or Out Novel

By Nina Malkin

- ❏ 6X: The Uncensored Confessions
- ❏ 6X: Loud, Fast, & Out of Control
- ❏ Orange Is the New Pink

By Jeanine Le Ny

- ❏ Once Upon a Prom: Date
- ❏ Once Upon a Prom: Dress
- ❏ Once Upon a Prom: Dream

MORE PRAISE FOR JONATHAN KELLERMAN AND HIS ALEX DELAWARE NOVELS

When the Bough Breaks
"An engrossing thriller . . . This knockout of an entertainment is the kind of book which establishes a career in one stroke."
—*New York Newsday*

Silent Partner
"A complex and haunting story of tangled personalities, deeply buried family secrets, and of violence lying thinly under the surface."
—*Los Angeles Times Book Review*

Time Bomb
"Virtually impossible to put aside until the final horrifying showdown."
—*People*

Private Eyes
"Spellbinding suspense . . . Unforgettable."
—*Houston Chronicle*

Devil's Waltz
"Reads like wildfire . . . Harrowing suspense."
—*The New York Times Book Review*

Please turn the page for more reviews. . . .

Bad Love

"*Bad Love* will have you looking over your shoulder before you turn out the lights."
—*Detroit Free Press*

Self-Defense

"Satisfying, suspenseful."
—*Playboy*

The Clinic

"Quite possibly the best of the series—and that's saying quite a lot."
—*Chicago Tribune*

Survival of the Fittest

"Why is it so hard to put down a Kellerman thriller. . . ? It's simple: the nonstop action leaves you breathless; the plot twists keep you guessing; the themes . . . are provocative."
—*Publishers Weekly*